KILL U

Chad Lehrmann

Didactic Cafe Press

Copyright © 2023 Chad Lehrmann

All rights reserved

The characters and events portrayed in this book are fictitious. Any similarity to real persons, living or dead, is coincidental and not intended by the author.

No part of this book may be reproduced, or stored in a retrieval system, or transmitted in any form or by any means, electronic, mechanical, photocopying, recording, or otherwise, without express written permission of the publisher.

Cover design by: Chad Lehrmann via Canva Pro
Printed in the United States of America

Academy.

Camden was a ten-year veteran, but one that had never had to pull his weapon. Until that morning. Part of the reason he never pulled his gun was his size. He was six foot four and built like Atlas. He waded into the woods with a fearlessness that only the truly tough men exuded.

Or the arrogant.

"Watch my six," Camden ordered. He was impatient with new recruits. Figured it was good for them to get tough love. His last two had made sergeant inside of two years, and Camden liked to think he was a big part of why they did. This Faust kid was greener than he liked, but he was about to get baptized in a big way.

"What's he look like?" Faust asked, swinging his shot gun toward a shaking pine branch.

"Swiss cheese, if what Sheriff Knox said is to be believed," Camden said gruffly. He snapped his head around toward a crunching noise, then chuckled to himself. Sullivan Knox was a small-town sheriff that had definitely got in over his head. And his town paid for it in blood. Camden thought as little of small-town sheriffs as he did of rookies. But a cop was a cop. And no one bled a boy in blue and expected to get away with it on Holt Camden's watch. "But Sergeant Volker gave me the BOLO when we headed here. It says he's early twenties with brown hair and brown eyes. 'Bout five eight or so."

"Sure it ain't me?" Faust joked, tousling his brown hair and pointing to his own brown eyes.

Camden turned slowly and looked Faust up and down, then snorted. "Don't pay to joke around with a murderer on the loose. I might get an itchy trigger finger," Camden said without humor.

Faust reacted by biting his lip and ducking his head, like a scolded puppy.

Camden turned around and pressed deeper into the woods. He came to an opening in the trees and he looked out across a lake. On the far side was a tall saw mill. Kingston's biggest landmark. And the escaped killer had come from it. "Gotta be around here somewhere," Camden said, kneeling down and seeing wet soil a few feet from the edge of the water. "Came this way. Getcher gun ready, kid. We get this boy and we get medals."

Camden rose and turned. Faust was gone. He snarled with disgust. "Kid, we gotta keep each other in sight."

"I agree," came a new voice- a muffled tone with a hint of a sneer.

Camden wheeled around looking for the sound of the voice. But it didn't come again. Faust was nowhere to be found. "Come out, Sean," Camden called. "Surrender yourself. It's the only way you make it out alive."

"I could say the same about you," came the muffled voice. But it was closer. Right behind Camden. He turned once more, and he was looking into a solid wall of foliage.

WARNINGS

This book contains intense violence and blood, as well as threatening language and scenery.

CHAPTER 1

A lone police cruiser sat beside the isolated road near Kingston, Texas. The red and blue lights splashed their light on the thick pine forest where two officers from Nacogdoches had entered a few minutes before.

They were among dozens of other officers from the surrounding area, responding to a call unlike any they had ever heard. A small town had been cut off from the rest of the world, and something evil had happened there. Six killers- or maybe seven, the reports were unclear- had turned Kingston into a bloody playground. Fires raged, bodies were strewn across streets and inside many buildings. And every single one of the killers was dead.

Except for one.

One was unaccounted for, and so a manhunt in the surrounding area had been called for. Officers Cade Faust and Holt Camden were slowly stalking through the dense wood, shotguns drawn, and looking for the final killer. A young man, reports suggested. His name was Sean, according to a witness' report, and the officers trusted that witness. He was one of their own. Sheriff Sullivan Knox had played a role in the capture and killing of the murderers, but he was on his way to a Dallas trauma center with life-threatening wounds. That made Faust and Camden dead serious about finding the man who hurt their proverbial brother in blue.

Faust was a rookie, his first day on the job, in fact. He had completed the Academy in Dallas just a month earlier and been called up by Nacogdoches PD just the week before. He'd done a virtual interview, what with the world still recovering from a pandemic and the fears that came with it. Small towns like Kingston ignored the distancing and masking, but the Nac was a bit more cautious. He'd just met his desk sergeant (a guy named Volker) and his new partner Camden about five minutes before the "all hands on deck" call went out.

Faust was an outsider in every sense of the word. He hailed from near Austin, not from East Texas. He was orphaned as a child when his single mother died in a car accident. With no father claiming him, Cade went into foster care, and won the lottery. He had great adoptive parents who instilled a strong desire for justice and a moral code. Unfortunately, when he was in college, they were killed in a home invasion. Cade decided then and there to pursue a career in law enforcement. He left college and enrolled in the Dallas Police

Two large, red eyes looked back at him.

And a saw-blade smile grinned back at him.

Camden jumped back, startled, and the face moved at him. He was so transfixed by the oddity of the mask that he almost didn't see the broken branch arcing toward his neck. When he did see it, it was too late. The branch tore into his jugular, just above his vest, and sprayed blood across the wooden mask as it smiled down on him with those dead red eyes. Camden gurgled as he choked on his own blood, dropping his shotgun and crumbling to the ground.

The man wearing the mask, the man who had once been Sean Densman, 'the Novice,' in the events of Killtown- stood over his latest victim, and pulled the branch from his throat. Behind the mask, Sean smiled, and his own eyes lit up. He brought the branch's jagged tip down again, and again, obliterating Holt Camden's face.

That was when Cade Faust came from behind a wall of green, wiping his mouth of the remnants of the nervous vomit he couldn't hold down any longer. His anxiety had driven him in shame to evacuate his stomach in privacy. It was why he hadn't responded to Camden's calls. Now he stood face to face with a killer. Wearing a wooden mask.

Instinct kicked in and Faust raised his shotgun and fired. The blast struck the assailant in the face, and splinters of wood and red glass sprayed outward from the killer's head. He fell backward and lay still.

Faust kept his gun trained on the figure laying on the ground as he walked over to check Camden. He was planning to check his pulse, but one look at the mess that was his brief partner's face told him it was pointless.

With one hand still on the gun, Faust reached to his radio with the other and called for an ambulance and backup. "I have the suspect wounded and on the ground. Officer Camden is dead, but I can hold the susp-"

Faust's legs went out from under him and he fell backward. The shotgun fired into the trees above, and the killer was on his feet. The mask was still on, but it was pitted and cracked from the shotgun blast. The red eyes were spider-webbed, with a constellation of holes. Blood was pouring from behind the mask, and a bloody hand reached up to his face to remove the mask.

The description of the killer was useless, Faust realized. The shotgun blast had torn the face apart, and yet somehow the man's eyes were intact. Brown eyes stared back at Faust from a red mass of hammered flesh. In those eyes was something like recognition. Or rage. It was difficult to tell.

Sean looked at the officer on the ground and went for their shotgun.

Faust read the killer's intent and clutched the weapon tightly, rising to meet the attacker. Their hands locked on the gun and they struggled for control. Faust could feel his stomach twisting as his face was just inches from the hamburger that had been a human visage just moments ago, but he knew he couldn't give even a bit. He couldn't understand how the man was still upright. A cursory glance would tell you he had numerous wounds on his body even before the blast to the face. Not only was he standing, he was somehow getting the upper hand on Faust.

"Give…ugh..up, Sean," Faust grunted.

What might have been a mouth twisted into a smile, exposing shattered teeth. "There is no Sean. Only the Host remains. And a good host returns the gifts of their guests." With a swift twist, Sean pulled the shotgun down and Faust felt a fire in his own face, followed by a deafening bang.

The world went black for a moment, then Faust saw the forest come back into focus. He felt no pain, but he knew that was shock- his face had taken a glancing blow from a shotgun at point-blank range. He focused in and saw the gun barrel now pointed directly at his head. He kicked, and caught his attacker in the shoulder, and the gun left Sean's hands. It fell just two feet from Faust. It was also two feet from Sean Densman.

The Host.

Both men saw their moment and went for the gun.

The tops of the trees came alive with birds fleeing the thunderous sound of another shotgun blast. Then all was silent.

For several minutes, there was an eerie silence in the woods across the lake from Kingston, Texas.

Then sirens and flashing light shook the silence and serenity to death. The ambulance slid to a stop, and two EMTs emerged, then paused, looking at each other with uncertainty. Should they enter the woods? There was a killer in there.

They made their decision when a figure stumbled out of the woods- a red wound where a face should be.

Wearing a police officer's uniform and holding a shotgun like a crutch. "I'm Officer Cade Faust," the figure mumbled. "The killer is dead…in there." Then he collapsed.

The EMT's went to work and managed to save Faust's life.

Camden had been right about one thing, after all.

Faust got a medal for ending the final villain of Killtown.

The game was over.

KILLTOWN: SEASON 2, EPISODE 1

It's not hyperbole to say that the murders in the small East Texas town of Kingston have proven to be the most shocking true crime story of the last decade. How could a sleepy town become the site of a serial killer competition? And all because of small town, family drama?

As your host in season one of Killtown, I, Rogan Benson, led you through the events of that blood-soaked evening, minute by minute. We met killers like Andy Keane, aka the Pyro. And Stew Lomax, the Wraith. It was this very podcast that uncovered the true identity of the Brute, one Wes Williams. Still no word on Mr. Blue's true identity, though. And of course, we learned the tragic story of the Novice, Sean Densman, who was intended to be the killer's sacrifice, but survived till the last. Until heroic rookie officer Cade Faust, suffering tremendous wounds himself, put the killer down.

So, where do we go now? In Season Two, we will explore where they are now. The survivors and heroes of the horrific tragedy. We all know that Lindsey Knox wrote a bestselling account of the harrowing night of horror. But what of daughter Amber, and the other heroic cop, Sullivan Knox? How have they fared since leaving Kingston? Kingston itself has become a bit of a character in this tale, as many survivors come out to tell stories that change our perspective of the sleepy little town.

Before we get to all that, we have a special guest with us. One of the survivors of the Battle of the Mill, as we call it here, the man who would become Sheriff, Mr. Claude Garvin!

CHAPTER 2

Claude Garvin smiled at the young man across from him in the sound booth, and adjusted his headset. Claude had lost a lot of weight, and gotten into decent shape since Killtown, having become a minor celebrity. He had been on nationwide morning talk shows, featured on several of those prime-time network true crime shows, and even appeared as a special guest on a couple reality TV shows.

He had to admit, he liked the fame.

And the little podcast he was sitting with now was a great example of the public's thirst for more on the sordid tale he had lived through. The podcast had started as a class project at the small university in Nacogdoches, King University. Yes, it was a college named for the same family that started Kingston, which was just about thirty miles away. Rogan Benson was a young journalism major with a good voice and a keen interest in true crime, so he decided to give the world of podcasting a shot. And why not use the

story that was literally so close to home? Rogan was an average sized guy with wavy brown hair and horn-rimmed glasses that framed his striking blue eyes perfectly. And which he only wore for the added 'academic effect.
He had a TV face even though he was on the 'radio,' as it were.

Claude wondered how long it would be before that changed.

Dateline and 48 Hours had done their own spins, what with their high production values and Keith Morrison's somber narration, and the people ate it up. But Rogan had two things they did not- proximity and something to prove. The kid had done a bang-up job of getting local survivors, even scoring an interview with Lindsey Knox, who had written the bestselling book about Killtown. That had been early on, before she and her family decided to try distancing themselves from the spectacle.

And with the Sullivans out of the spotlight, it fell on Claude Garvin. The self-proclaimed Red-Neck Sheriff of East Texas.

"Why, thanks fer havin' me back, Rogan," Claude replied to his introduction. "Always a pleasure."

"How is Kingston these days?" Rogan asked, his brown eyes wide as he waited for Claude to regale him. "Especially with the third anniversary coming up?"

"We got a big ole deal planned," Claude

explained. "We small-town folk like to honor our fallen. We like to look back on our heroes and lift 'em up, as it were. The Baptist Church is having a celebration for Bob Atkins in their new building. They are officially calling it the Bob Atkins Memorial Fellowship Hall, and that day is the... forgive my crossin' of denominations, christenin' of the Hall."

"And what about you, Sheriff? You being honored as well?"

Claude smiled. "Now, I don't like to toot my own horn," he lied- because he loved to do just that. "But yeah, they're gonna name a street after me. And I get to be the Master a Ceremonies for the whole shindig. And, I'm gettin' a plaque with my name on it at City Hall, for Meritorious Service. Can ya imagine that?"

Rogan laughed, and then said, "I definitely can! No one has done more in the last year for Kingston than you, sir. Not even the Knox family. By the way, have you spoken with the former Sheriff Sully Knox?"

For the first time, Claude's smile faded. No matter what he did, Claude would never be anything more than Sully's sidekick. He was getting the honors he was because Sully refused them. Claude was the fall back. The consolation prize. And Sully had made it clear that he was not a fan of the attention.

"Not in a bit, no," Claude said. "He and Lindsey and their girl really wanted ta get away from Killtown- and Kingston. So, I say, live and let live. Some folks just don't like diggin' up bodies- if you'll furgive my pun?"

"Speaking of that," Rogan said, shifting in his seat, and his own mood changing. "There have been concerns that all the attention the events of Killtown have gotten might lead to copycats. More killers like Jane Sharp and Nate Clupe trying to replicate the contest. What are your thoughts?"

Claude sighed. "Naw, ain't nobody gonna try that again. Those two were all kinds of messed up, and besides, all the players in it are dead. And besides *that*, if anyone did try to make a go of it again, I'd be ready for them." Claude gave Rogan thumbs up and a wink. He missed Rogan's subtle eye roll altogether.

◆ ◆ ◆

Claude walked out of the building that housed the podcast studio, a red brick building on King University's campus that was home to several audio-visual labs. Although Rogan's podcast was syndicated and he made good money from it, he still used University resources to save money when he could. The kid was resourceful in that way. Claude admired the kid's initiative and savvy.

"You need to be careful, Claude," came a deep voice from the side of the building.

Claude turned to see Sullivan "Sully" Knox leaning against the building. He had aged more than one should have in just three years. Gray had crept onto the sidewalls of his hair, more lines and creases appeared around his eyes, and he had one shoulder that sunk a tad lower than the other- a wound from three years earlier. One of many.

"Aw, Sully, it ain't hurtin' no one," Claude replied. "Sides, you know a sheriff's salary ain't nothin' to write home about."

Sully half- smiled and stood up from the wall. He walked over to Claude, a slight hitch in his step. "No, no, it isn't. But dredging up this part of the past is dangerous. I know you don't think anyone will try to copy it, but the fact is, there have been rumors-"

"Sully, just own up that you don't like me gettin' the spotlight," Claude interrupted. "Ya jest can't take it, me getting the interviews. Fact is, you never wanted me to be a cop, no how. Only reason ya deputized me was Killtown. So, now I take pride in my job. Besides, you left, Kingston. I stayed."

Sully sighed. "I did leave. And you know why, too. The town didn't want us there anymore. They blamed us for the killings, because Jane was doing it to get back at my dad. My family. And they hated that Lindsey wrote that book, too."

Claude chuckled dryly. "So did you."

"Fair," Sully replied. "But she wasn't a fan of my keeping things from her. We worked it out. Well, we are *working* it out. Lindsey has her job teaching here now and loves it. And, well, being head of campus security isn't so bad, either."

Claude could sense that Sully was softening, and asked, "So, how's Amber doin' with ya'll being here?"

Now Sully chuckled. "She's studying criminology, of all things. Got a good group of friends, for the most part. Actually, she's gotten close with Rogan up there. He's been kind enough to keep from bugging her about doing an interview."

"So, you really have moved on, Sully?" Claude asked.

Sully was quiet for a moment. Then he answered, "As best we can. But does anyone ever really get over something like what we went through?"

CHAPTER 3

Knox sat patiently in the waiting room of the psychiatrist's office. Since the murders and all that they brought up, he had been in therapy. All three members of the Knox family had been. Individually, as a whole, and he and Lindsey as a couple. Lindsey hadn't liked that Knox knew things about his family and hadn't shared- namely the dark secrets about his father and unknown sister. Knox didn't like that Lindsey wrote the book on...the murders. He hated to use the name, Killtown, because it was what *they* had called it. The killers. She said it was to process her feelings and experiences, and he was fine with that. But then she published it.

The book was a hit, and then interviews came. Distance between them grew because Lindsey was doing press, and he got roped into a few interviews. And he hated interviews. The book had enabled them to pay off some debts and pay for Amber's college. Then the job offer came.

For Lindsey.

Knox was an afterthought. King University was so small it didn't really need much security, but it did need publicity. So, they created his position, which was basically that of a glorified security guard with a desk.

They took it because Kingston had made it clear that the Knox family was no longer welcome. The people blamed Knox's family for bringing the evil to their town. "Why didn't you accept Jane Sharp into your family?" was asked often. Then they asked him to resign as Sheriff, then the School Board hinted strongly that they were not going to renew Lindsey's contract. The message was transparent.

Knox had never imagined leaving his hometown permanently, but now that they had, he felt free. Free to start over. Free to make a new life.

He had only really come to accept that because of the therapy with Dr. Van S. Crewe. Crewe was younger than Sully and Lindsey, a characteristic that had both Lindsey and Knox balking at first. But he asked good questions, pushed in the right ways, and had actually helped them tremendously. The trust in their relationship was returning, but it was still fragile. As for his personal struggles, Knox would say he was coming to terms with his new reality.

A reality where he was a washed-up police officer who got a pity job because the university really wanted to hire his wife.

Lindsey walked in to the waiting room, and she gave Knox a smile. She sat next to him and kissed him on the lips and said, "How's your day?"

"Good, saw Claude," Knox said. It was strange, but after what happened in Kingston, it was small talk that had become most difficult to them. She had felt he hid his true thoughts and feelings behind it, and he felt it was her way of avoiding a confrontation. They had grown distant, but when she took the job at the university, it had been Knox that suggested they take advantage of the counseling they offered as a part of health benefits. It had saved their marriage, truth be told.

The door opened behind the desk, and a young man walked out. He had blonde hair and blue eyes and wore a green Henley. "Hey, Asher," Lindsey said as he looked at them. Asher Hunter was Dr. Crewe's intern. He was a junior psych major at the college, and a member of Amber's friend group as well.

"Ah, Mr. and Mrs. Knox. The doctor will be ready for you in a moment," Asher said grinning. "Amber coming today?"

Lindsey smiled, a smile that communicated to Knox that she knew why Asher asked that question. "Not today, just a marital counseling session today."

Asher shrugged, but even Knox could see the disappointment on his face. The kid had a thing for Amber. Great.

From outside came the sound of shouts, and Knox turned to the window just a few feet away. He could see a crowd gathering around the red brick building next door- the home of Rogan Benson's podcast. There were signs waving, reading things like "Keep Smut Out of Our University" and "Don't Glorify Violence." Knox was particularly disdainful of the one that indicated which group it was: 'Keep Our Airways Pure.'

A local woman named Nikki Meyers was hellbent on shutting down anything she deemed inappropriate, especially that which she labeled as 'smut.' It had a broad definition, that word, when used by Meyers. From pornography to violence to even some children's cartoons. Knox wondered if she even knew what 'smut' meant.

"You have to deal with that?" Lindsey asked.

Dr. Crewe poked his head out of his office and asked, "Sully, Lindsey, you ready?"

Knox watched as uniformed officers from the local police department arrived and began to take up positions on the crowd. He felt a moment of disappointment at the realization that he wasn't needed. "Nah, the cops have it," he said, masking his feelings. "We're ready, Doc."

◆ ◆ ◆

Rogan Benson walked down the steps and stopped at the glass door that led to the street. A mob of about twenty people were standing there, as they did from time to time, shouting and waving signs that called for the ending of his show. And sure enough, right there in the middle of the crowd was Nikki Meyers.

She was just south of what Rogan would call middle-aged, attractive in a stern way. Her hair was a bit too big and her clothing a bit too fashionable to make her look like a stereotypical 'stern librarian' trope, but her mannerisms were all about judgment and condescension. He knew she was married, but he had never met the husband. And still, he pitied the man.

Rogan waved teasingly at Nikki through the glass door, then stepped out. "Good day, Nikki, getting a little protesting in before yoga class, I see."

She scrunched her face in a manner that was altogether unappealing. "You glorify violence and murder, and have the audacity to mock me?" She turned to her group. "You see, it is this sort of callousness that is ruining our youth today. It is all snark and sarcasm. Get the soundbite rather than substance."

Rogan tapped her on the shoulder. "Isn't that what you just did, too? Give your people a soundbite?"

She wheeled around with a glare and a snort, and her finger was in Rogan's face. "Do you ever consider the pain you cause the victims by dredging this up again and again? Those murders should be forgotten!"

Rogan sighed, then scanned the crowd. Local people of the more...traditional type were there to support Nikki. Mothers from the PTO and retired old men who were either drug there by their wives or just wanting something to be angry about. He even saw one of the local ministers, a fire and brimstone old school guy named Felix Casey. Casey was almost as much of a thorn in Rogan's side as Nikki. "You must repent of your sinful ways, boy, or ye shall burneth in HELL!" Casey shouted with wild eyes and flying spittle. Rogan wondered why all old school preachers like that resorted to King James when essentially cursing people.

He saw the cops were standing around, and one officer gave a disinterested shrug as if to say 'What can we do? Free speech an all, kid.'

Rogan began to feel like he was being watched. He knew all the eyes of the 'Keep Our Airways Pure' folks were on him, but this felt different. He nervously looked around but saw nothing out of order. Just people leaving their offices and trying to avoid the scene that had become an all too frequent traffic concern.

"Well, what do you have to say for yourself, Mr. Benson?" Nikki was demanding.

"I consider that every time I do a podcast," he said, his good nature disappearing. "It's why I am profiling survivors. And you seem keen on judging me for making a modest profit off of my podcast, while you seem to enjoy some benefits, as well."

Nikki's jaw dropped in an overly rehearsed, offended expression. "Excuse me?"

Rogan shrugged. "Look around you. You wouldn't matter one bit in this world if you hadn't found some cause, some excuse to rile people up. If you really think we should be doing better to respect the victims of Killtown, maybe don't make a spectacle of your protests. Have a good day." He forced himself through the crowd, nodded as one officer gave him a wink of approval, and crossed the street.

But that feeling that there had been someone watching him remained. He looked back toward the buildings and the crowd, but saw nothing.

◆ ◆ ◆

"I think we're making good progress," Dr. Crewe said, taking his seat at his desk. "But I want to hear what you two think." He leaned back, wearing a casual suit with a button-down shirt and no tie. He had board straight brown hair, parted on one side and just a bit long on the other. His mouth was small, and he kept it in a tight, small line until he smiled, then his whole face would light up. At that moment, there was no hint of a smile.

Lindsey and Knox exchanged a look, and

then Lindsey spoke. "I was so angry at Sully for not telling me about his family secrets. In our whole marriage, he had never done that. I can see now why he did it. He was intending to shield me, to protect me. When I was principal of Kingston High, it was a high-profile job in a small town. As we see now, secrets like that would have cost me my job. Really, well, they did."

"Sully? What say you?"

"I should have told her, I see that now," he said. "And I see that Lindsey's choice to write the book was not her way of retaliating against me, it was her way of processing...what happened." Dr. Crewe shifted in his seat and looked intently at Knox. "Yeah, yeah, I know. Our relationship is good again, after a long time. But I still have some issues. I mean, what I went through-"

"Lindsey and Amber being kidnapped, held at the point of a knife and a gun, then you almost dying?" Dr. Crewe interjected. "Yeah, that's a lot. It was a lot for Lindsey and Amber, too. But where I think they have been successful at moving on, you seem stuck. You can't even say 'Killtown,' can you?"

Knox looked at Crewe, his lips a tense, thin line. As if opening his mouth too much would let that very word out into the world to wreak chaos. "Why do I need to?"

Lindsey gripped his hand tightly and said, "Because it changed you. It took a lot more than just your health from you. It took your job, your hometown, and even more than that, it took your identity. You were a hometown hero, and then a pariah. Now, you work here, largely behind a desk when you are a 'get out and pound the pavement' kinda cop."

"And it's a pity job, at that," Knox said sullenly.

Crewe looked up at Knox. "Now, why do you say that? Don't you think King University needs a security force? I mean, *I* appreciate your presence here."

Knox grimaced. "One gimpy retired cop is not a security force. And no, I don't think King University needs me. They need Lindsey- but I'm just the tag along."

"Every university, even small ones like this, have a security presence," Crewe replied. "Why do you think King U doesn't?"

Knox sighed. "Look around you. Outside of that podcast Rogan Benson does, nothing bad ever happens here." Knox looked down at his feet. "Nothing ever happens here, period."

CHAPTER 4

Officer Charlie Volker sat in the dim glow of the solitary overhead light in his cage and stared at the computer screen. He was directly in front of two doors that led out to the entryway of the metal building that housed all of Nacogdoches' PD's evidence. Aside from a few meeting rooms up front, the bulk of the building was the large warehouse in which Charlie spent most of his time.

He was reading the weather for the weekend, when he planned a trip to Lake Nacogdoches for some fishing. Charlie was a middle-aged man, single and proud of it, with a small gut from drinking too much on his off time. Since he had transferred over to the evidence clerk job from being a desk sergeant, he had been able to plan his off time with certainty, and he missed nothing about being a beat cop. He got to sit on his butt and read mystery novels, watch old sporting events online, and had gotten fantastic at solitaire. He only cheated once in a while.

Plus, Charlie got to chat with the detectives

who dropped in to register and log evidence. A lot of them had been officers on the beat with him, then those under his charge. Everyone makes different life choices, though. And while they were still out there solving crimes, Charlie was making sure the evidence they collected was secure. For instance, Detective Joshua Joel had been Charlie's partner about twenty years earlier. Joel had become a detective after two years of riding together. Now, Joel was a near celebrity in the department.

Charlie Volker was a clerk.

And Charlie was okay with that.

Clerks didn't get shot at or stabbed or attacked.

Joel had walked in and waved at his old friend, followed by a younger man dressed in a blue button-down shirt and black slacks. Joel had brown hair, graying around the temples, and was not a huge man. His blue eyes were ringed by lines from squinting into the Texas sun and at the intricacies of crime scenes too much. His new partner had brown hair and brown eyes, but what struck Charlie was the scarring. The man had pockmark scars all over his face, along with straight line marks around the sides of his face. He was still a handsome man, but he had clearly had reconstructive surgery at some point. His brown eyes searched the darkened room widely, like a scared animal that thought he was being hunted.

"Charlie, my boy, meet Cade Faust, my new

partner," Joel said with a smile. "Wanted to show him down here to the evidence locker on his first day. How you been, buddy?"

Charlie appreciated that Joshua Joel treated him like an equal. It made him feel good. "Keepin' busy, Joshua. Ya know how it is," Charlie replied, eyeing Faust and trying to place that name. "First day, detective?"

Faust nodded. "Yeah, just got assigned to Detective Joel today. He's been showing all around."

"Joel's a great partner, kid, you're lucky to have 'em," Charlie said. Then the switch clicked. "Say, you ain't the Faust that took down that last Killtown killer, are ya?"

Faust ducked his head and bit his lip, then answered sheepishly, "Yeah, but I honestly don't like to talk about it. Don't remember much- just going into the woods and then waking up on the stretcher being carried out."

Charlie felt a bit of embarrassment for the kid. He was a hero and had no memory of what made him one. "Oh, sorry," he said.

Faust shrugged. "No worries. You couldn't know how I felt about it all."

"Thanks, kid," Charlie said, truly grateful for the kindness. "Ya know, those masks are here in evidence. You ever want ta take a look, just let me know."

An almost imperceptible twitch went across Faust's face, but Charlie saw it. It was the twitch one has when they realize something that terrifies them might be in the room with them. Joel changed the subject to ask about Charlie's plans for the week. They chatted for about five more minutes, Faust not saying much, but interjecting from time to time.

When the two detectives left, Charlie checked his watch. It was a quarter to six. He watched a few YouTube videos on how to make your own lures for bass fishing, then went and heated his dinner. He read from his book and might have dozed off for a moment.

Nacogdoches had crime, but it was not a daily occurrence to have evidence brought in to be logged. So, cat naps were a thing. He checked his watch again. It was eight-thirty.

There was only one window in the evidence locker, and it was a transom high up on the western wall. A quick glance told Charlie it was decidedly dark out. His shift ran to midnight, when he would do a last sweep for the night and the overnight shift came in then. He reached for the book again and leaned back in his chair.

Then he heard the sound of movement behind him, in the stacks of evidence.

A chill ran down his spine, because if a detective came in and caught him napping, he was done for. The book slid from his fingers and slapped down on the floor beneath the desk.

Charlie stood and ambled toward the sound of cardboard boxes being moved off metal shelves.

When he heard plastic evidence bags fall to the ground, he knew it wasn't a detective. He pulled his service revolver as a cold sweat broke out on his upper lip and across his forehead.

Someone had broken in.

He turned the corner and saw a figure clad in black from head to toe standing over a table. The figure's back was turned to Charlie, but he could tell they were wearing a long black cloak or- was that a cape? It was tattered at the edges, almost like it had been in a fire and was partially consumed by the flames. There was a metallic clang as something the figure removed from the box was set upon the table. Charlie shifted his gaze to it and immediately recognized what it was.

The metal mask worn by the Killtown murderer called the Brute.

Looking to the floor by the intruder's feet, Charlie saw a clown mask. Mr. Blue's.

"You should have stayed asleep," a muffled and augmented voice emanated from the dark shape.

Charlie looked back to the figure, who turned slowly to reveal that it was wearing a mask.

It was wooden, burned to bring out the grain, with a metal saw blade smile. Cracked red, bulbous circles stared at Charlie, with blackened, burned eyebrows and buckshot holes providing accents. Dark brown blood stains were scattered on the face.

Charlie was staring at the Host.

They were both frozen for a moment- Charlie out of fear, the intruder in anticipation. Almost like a western gunfighter waiting to see was the quickest draw. Testing his mettle. The wooden face tilted to the side ever-so-slightly, then he whipped his wrist out from his hip.

Charlie barely had time to react as the glint of a steel blade caught in the dim light before the hilt of the knife crushed his nose. His gun hand dropped to his side as his other hand shot to his nose- and the intruder was rushing at him, a second knife already drawn.

Charlie tried to bring his revolver up, but the attacker was too quick- the blade slashed out and cut his wrist. His fingers went numb, and the gun clattered to the ground. Charlie released his nose and tried to throw a punch at the wooden mask, but the intruder blocked his blow. He felt the air leave his lungs as a knee shot into his stomach. Charlie stumbled back into the wall, and the attacker advanced, tilting his head once more as he juggled the bloody knife.

Then the figure spoke. "I must make a decision, officer. Do I kill you, and leave a note in your blood? Or do I let you live, so that you can tell everyone that the Host has returned? What do you think?"

Charlie spat blood at the man's feet, then summoned any courage he had to say defiantly, "Screw you, mother-"

The Host swung the knife out and slashed

across Charlie's throat, literally cutting off his curse. The cop began to gurgle, as both hands- including the dead one- went to his throat. His eyes were wide and his breathing turned to a ragged gasp as he sank to his knees before the man who was taking his life. The Host knelt down so that they were eye to plastic eye. That head tilted again, and slowly, methodically, he raised the knife and pressed the blade into Charlie's left shoulder. A gurgling scream tried to make its way out of his mouth, but instead simply produced a blood bubble.

The Host removed the knife, then repeated the action on the other shoulder. Blurred vision was affecting Charlie and his eyes had become glassy. His blinks became longer, and finally, as the blade was removed once more, they closed forever.

"Message in blood it is," the Host said, stabbing the blade into his macabre flesh inkwell.

❖ ❖ ❖

Amber Knox sat on the green couch, sipping her coffee in the eclectic atmosphere of the Loco Mocha coffee shop.

Until she came to college earlier that fall, she had never been a coffee drinker. But now, she was decidedly addicted. It was why she sat drinking her latte at nearly ten o'clock on a Tuesday. Well, she didn't have her Wednesday criminology class until eleven, so a late night was no big deal.

And the company was good.

Seated next to her was her roommate, Olivia "Liv" Fuentes. Liv was tall and slender, facts accented by her tendency to dress in all black. She had long black hair with blue streaks throughout and adorned her eyes with blue and black eyeshadow that stood out starkly from her honey-colored skin. She frequently declared she was not, in fact, a goth, but Amber wondered. Her dark toned apparel belied the truth that Liv was a genuinely kind person. Even if she never actually smiled. And she was an aggressive activist.

Next to Liv was Dex Smalley. Dex was tall and muscular, a star of the basketball team at King University. His black hair was close cropped and the deep brown skin of his face was clean shaven. He looked more like a high schooler than a college sophomore. Unlike a lot of jocks that Amber had encountered, he was humble, kind, and brilliant as well.

In the chair across from Amber sat Mikey Brooks. She too played basketball for the King University Lions, but where Dex was an average height point guard, Mikey was a six-foot two center with flaming red hair. She was the extroverted organizer of many of the group's activities and had been the brains behind the run to the coffee shop.

Asher Hunter was there, too, next to Mikey. He was a junior, and even though he was the intern at her psychiatrist's office, he never spoke of her visits there. She was eternally grateful for his discretion. She also suspected it was partly due to his not-insignificant crush on her.

The final member of their group- at least of those present- was Margot Lucas. She was a sorority girl, and one of those young people that was either so likable that she could belong to drastically different circles or so vapid that she had no personality of her own. Amber was not sure which she was.

They were a diverse group, at least in terms of their extracurricular activities. But there was one thing they had in common. All were in that criminology class Amber had the next morning. Their group had started as a study team, but there had been an instant connection. Amber had long ago given up any hope for anonymity, especially with her mom's book and Rogan Benson's podcast. The group had taken her presence with a shrug, and then they fell into a rhythm of friendship that was safe and comfortable. On rare occasions, someone had said something about Killtown, there had been a moment of awkward silence, then they moved on.

It wasn't that Amber didn't want to talk about it. Actually, quite the opposite. She wanted to talk. She had dealt with her tragedy- watching her boyfriend murdered before her eyes and seeing her father almost killed. Her own role in the final showdown with the Hosts- sledgehammering her own recently discovered aunt to buy time for her father and mother to save her- had turned her into some sort of 'final girl' heroine in the eyes of many. She was okay with that. Welcomed it, even.

Amber Knox had made a decision in the aftermath of Killtown to never be a victim again. She knew part of fulfilling that self-prophecy was speaking out. And doing it loudly.

"Did you see President Straub announce a tuition hike?" Liv asked.

Dex and Mikey shrugged. "Nah, how much?" Dex asked.

"I heard it's almost ten percent," Asher said. "My question is, where is that money going? Your mom getting a raise, Amber?"

Amber had been in her own world when she heard her name. Her mind had been listening enough for her to know the question, and she replied, "Doubtful. Dad won't either."

Amber noted several sideways glances. Her friends were not fans of her dad. Several had gotten tickets for parking improperly. They all thought he was a glorified meter maid, but Amber didn't let it get to her. She knew the kind of man her dad was. And even if he had hidden the fact that Jane Sharp was his half-sister from the family, it had been for good reason.

"It's not like most of you will notice, outside Asher, Amber and me," Liv said, a hint of teasing disgust in her voice.

"What's that supposed to mean," Margot

asked. "Because my daddy has money? You're just trying to lean into your 'victim' role again, honey." The last jab was a joke- mostly.

Liv glared in jest and shrugged. "Well, let's be honest. You do have money, Dex and Mikey are on scholarship, and the final member of our group? Well, he certainly isn't worried about money. Not after what I heard today."

Mikey sat up. "Did he get it? Did they really offer it?"

"There's someone else who would know better. Right Amber?" Liv cut a sideways glance at her.

Amber felt her cheeks flush. They all knew she had a crush on the last member of the group, and he entered the coffee shop before she had to answer.

Rogan Benson came in, his long brown hair parted down the middle and sweeping across his cheeks. He wore his customary khaki sport coat that he said made him feel like a real journalist and had a leather briefcase strapped across his shoulder. He smiled broadly, then made eye contact with Amber, and she blushed even more.

"Dude, is it for real?" Dex asked. "Did the producers offer you a deal for a Killtown documentary?"

Rogan's smile grew even larger. "Yep! Got the papers in here!" he said, patting the leather case.

The group erupted in cheers and hugs.

Rogan had taken the criminology course merely to add more professional flavor and verbiage to the Killtown podcast, but he had eschewed any attempt by other classmates or the professor to play on that borderline fame he possessed.

What Amber appreciated the most was that he had never pressured, let alone asked, for an exclusive from the one Killtown survivor no one had ever heard directly from.

So, she volunteered.

Amber hung back from the crowd a bit, but Rogan saw her and moved toward her. He gave her a hug, and even though she told herself it was totally platonic, her heart tried to convince her otherwise. Rogan was a junior, and with the documentary deal, he was probably not too long for King University. But there was the fact that her interview was the cornerstone of the documentary, so they would still get to see each other. Maybe then something could develop.

"Thank you," he said. "They loved the angle you pitched me. Hearing the story from your side was fresh and new. I can't wait to work with you on this!" His eyes twinkled, and Amber's heart again fluttered at the hope of a romantic glint in those irises. "What do your parents think about it?"

Amber bit her lip and was about to sheepishly explain that they had no idea when the sound of sirens pierced the reverie. Blue and red lights- lots of them- raced past the window.

"What's going on?" Margot asked.

Phones began to chirp all around the coffee shop. Amber pulled out her phone and saw a campus safety text. It read: "Shelter in place, possibly armed suspect is on the loose near campus." For a moment, Amber felt a shudder run through her body.

Asher piped up, "Socials are saying something about the evidence warehouse downtown. That's just a few blocks away."

They all exchanged a look, then bolted out the door as a unit.

CHAPTER 5

Cade Faust stepped out of his car and flashed his badge at the officer holding the tape. It was hard to believe he had just been there a few hours ago, before the white tin walls were bathed in red and blue lights and dozens of uniformed officers were milling about. He saw Detective Joel, who waved him over. Cade jogged to his partner.

"What do we do, boss?" Cade asked.

Joel sighed, and Cade saw sadness in his eyes. "We wait for them to get him down," he said, nodding back to the entrance of the warehouse.

Charlie Volker's body was tied up to the wall, spread eagled. He would have been almost unseen if not for the police lights. The security lights around the building were out, and the electricity to the building also seemed to have been cut. Cade turned and saw a gathering crowd just outside of the police line. "Should we go in, maybe see what's going on inside? I mean, he wasn't killed there, right?" Cade asked.

Joel smiled sadly. "Yeah. Yeah, that's a good idea," he rubbed his forehead. "Sorry, Charlie was a friend, as you know. Yeah, let's go in."

They passed beneath the fire truck ladder that extended its bucket up to Charlie's body. There were two crime scene techs hoisted above in order to take pictures before removing the body. Cade looked up and saw a thin blood trail running down the wall, slowly making its way to the metal lip over the doors. He made himself look away. Not because the blood upset him- he had seen plenty of death even as an officer. Mostly car accidents. No, it was that the blood was from a man he had just met. A nice man, a cop like him. Someone Cade Faust felt a connection with- slight as it was.

Joel flicked on his flashlight as they entered the dark building, and Cade copied that action. There was a definite blood trail, and they were following it back toward the evidence lockers themselves. On either side of them were doors that led to restrooms (on the right) and observation rooms (on the left). Straight ahead was the desk where they had met Charlie that afternoon.

It was in much the same state it had been in earlier, save for the book that lay on the floor beneath the desk. Cade noted it was an old dime store mystery novel, one Charlie had probably read a dozen times before. Well, someone had. It was washed out and the pages were yellowed with age. Well loved, you might say.

"Goes back this way," Joel said, moving into

the stacks of cardboard boxes on metal shelves.

The trail made a sharp left, but Cade noticed small black spots on the ground next to a gun-Charlie's. Probably blood spatter, Cade assumed. He moved the beam of his flashlight to the left and saw a wall covered in blood. Thick, dark pools had collected at the baseboard, arcing out unevenly toward their feet. Clear drag marks from the center of the pool indicated where Charlie's body had been dragged out. "How did they get him up on the top of the building without being seen?" Joel asked. "Someone had to pass by..."

"They shot out the streetlights and killed the ones in here," Cade said. "When I drove up, the only reason I could see anything was the lights from the patrol cars and fire truck." He turned back around to look down the aisle. "He must have seen the perp down there, with that box." Cade began to walk toward the box.

"First day and you're reading the scene like a pro," Joel said, following Cade down the aisle. "This seems like a lot of violence for a thief who got caught breaking in an evidence locker. Think it could be a drug thing, kid?"

Cade reached the cardboard box and froze. His light hit on a piece of metal, rounded like a helmet. He reached into his pocket and pulled out rubber gloves, shuffling the flashlight under his arms as he did. Once gloved up, he moved the helmet, and jumped back with a yelping curse.

"What is it?" Joel said, moving to look.

"Oh…" he said, then looked down to the side of the box where the case number and pertinent information was. "Metal helmet, clown mask… yep. It's from the Kingston deal." Joel moved his light toward Cade's face, which had turned a deathly shade of white. "You okay, kid?"

Cade shook his head in the affirmative, but he had seen more than the mask. He had seen a wooden face. In his mind's eye, a memory had risen up from the depths. A horrendous, red eyed wooden face. Even before Joel read the evidence tag, Cade had known what that box was from.

Killtown.

His darkest day.

So far.

"I-is there a wooden mask in there?" Cade asked.

Joel moved some things around in the box and then looked down at the tag. "Says there's supposed to be one, but it's not here."

Cade felt his stomach churn. He bolted out of the evidence locker and down the hall, bursting into the slightly cool night air, just as they were lowering Charlie down. He looked up and once again saw that trail of blood. But as he followed it to the spot where Charlie had been, any hope of keeping his dinner down was gone. The blood trail led to four words that sent waves of terror over Cade Faust.

I'm Back
-The Host

◆ ◆ ◆

Amber stared at the words written in blood.

"It can't be..." she whispered under her breath.

Asher was standing next to her and glanced over. "It's gotta be a copycat, Amber," he said, attempting to reassure her. He smiled.

It didn't work.

She took a deep breath and closed her eyes. She began to count down from ten and got to five when she felt a hand on her back. Amber opened her eyes and saw Rogan standing next to her. His presence *did* calm her, if only a bit. "This...this is strange. I mean, I sign the contract today and this happens?" He was in a sort of daze, out of it, in shock. "This'll really make the documentary folks happy."

Amber looked at him, her eyes wide. She knew he didn't mean it like he said it- or she hoped, anyway. But he seemed not to notice at all. She kept glaring at him, and finally he seemed to catch on.

"Wait- I didn't mean- ugh, I'm sorry," he stumbled. "I just meant that...never mind. I'll stop talking."

Amber smiled despite herself. He was a goofball, but a charming one nonetheless. He returned the smile, then said, "It's probably just the anniversary coming up. Or the podcast. It's not about you."

"The podcast would be *little* about him," Asher said under his breath. Rogan glared at him.

The rest of their group was standing there as well, trying to get a glimpse of the scene. Mikey, Liv, and Dex were a little further behind her, Rogan and Asher. Margot had broken away to join a pack of sorority sisters and their frat boyfriends.

Amber's mind was racing, and she realized she needed to call her parents. They needed to know. Preferably, before they saw it on the news. She pulled out her cell and called her dad.

"Amber, you okay?" her father's worried voice answered.

She sighed. "Dad, someone was killed tonight. A cop. Th-there was a note…"

Her father didn't immediately reply, so she forced herself to continue. "It said, *I'm Back* and it was signed… *the Host.*"

Silence.

"Dad?"

"Where?"

"At the…um, I think evidence warehouse for the police," she said, standing on her tiptoes and trying to see the signage.

"It is," Rogan confirmed, being tall enough to actually see it.

"On my way." *Click.*

"Your dad coming?" Asher asked.

"Yeah, I guess he should be here," she said.

She didn't want him to come, but she knew he would. Amber hadn't protested. She knew he had been miserable since the move and that he hated his new job. He felt unneeded. Neither she nor her mother had given him any reason to think that, at least, she didn't think they had. But it was on his face every time she saw him lately. He still walked with a slight limp from Killtown, but she knew his real injury was in his head. He blamed himself, even if he had convinced Dr. Crewe he was okay. Deep down, Amber felt that the shrink knew her father was putting up front. But she also knew the facade couldn't last.

Amber was proud of her father, he was still her hero. And so was her mother. She knew that Lindsey Knox writing the book had caused some strain in the family at first, but Amber was so glad she had written it. Not only did it set the family up financially, but it had also been the real therapy for her mother. In the same way, she hoped the documentary would be therapeutic for her.

If she could survive telling her parents she was doing it.

"Amber, are you okay?" Liv called out as she and Dex broke through the throng of people and reached her.

"Yeah," she said, mustering her confidence again. "It probably has nothing to do with me and my family. Do we know who it was? Who it was that died?"

"It was the evidence officer," came a reply

from a woman standing near the police line. The tone was dismissive and condescending, and when she turned, Amber's stomach sank.

Nikki Meyers looked down her nose at Amber. "Well, if it isn't that writer's daughter," she said, then noticed Rogan. "And with the podcaster." She snorted. "Wouldn't put it past you two to have pulled this for a shot at some fame."

Rogan turned toward her and Amber saw a flash of genuine rage cross his face. He was normally so calm and collected, so Amber was a bit taken aback. "You can picket outside the studio all you want, Nikki, but accusing me- and Amber- of murder is a step too far. Take it back."

Nikki narrowed her eyes beneath her dyed blonde bangs and her mouth twisted into a smile that was at once pained and angry and sadistic. "What, did I insult your refined sensibilities? Maybe you didn't kill him, but you are guilty of inciting this violence. Your podcast- and your mother's book- celebrated murder. And now, here is more murder. So, maybe you need to think about what you do with your platform a little more."

"And you need to think very carefully about your next words," Amber heard herself say. "For someone who hates what Rogan does so much, you sure seem to enjoy hanging on every word he says." She paused, then her own little smile crossed her face as she added a parting taunt. "Your husband know you got a little crush?"

Nikki Meyers' face flushed and her mouth

gaped open. "How dare you?!? Your parents should be ashamed of themselves for raising such a despicable child!"

"And yet, we couldn't be more proud," Lindsey Knox said, walking through the crowd with Sully. "Nikki, maybe you should make your way home." It was not a suggestion, and Amber was briefly reminded of hearing that same tone when her mother was a high school principal.

Nikki glared, then turned and moved away, shoving her way through the crowd.

"Man, the Knox women are fierce," Rogan said.

"Don't I know it," Knox said with a smile. "Rogan, Asher. I think you boys might also want to head home. Same for you guys," he said nodding at Mikey, Liv, and Dex.

"Yessir," Dex said with a nod.

"Dex," Knox said, placing a hand on his shoulder. "Make sure the young ladies get home safe. In fact, why don't you all head out together?" He looked up at the note in blood on the wall. "I think this might be just the beginning."

Asher nodded, "Yes sir. You guys be safe, too."

Rogan glanced back at Amber, and gave a subtle wink. She felt her cheeks flush.

Knox saw it, too.

"Amber, are you okay?" Lindsey asked, putting her arms around her daughter.

"Yeah, she's just a blowhard," Amber said.

"I meant about *that*," Lindsey said, indicating the crime scene.

"Oh, um, yeah, I guess," she said. "Rogan thinks it's not about us at all, probably just the podcast. And the fact that the anniversary is coming up."

"Oh, *Rogan* thinks, huh?" Knox asked, affecting an overly dramatic concerned father's face.

"*Dad!*" she whisper-shouted playfully.

Knox smiled, then he looked at the building. The smile faded. He walked up to the police line, and called out to a man in a blue suit standing next to a younger man who looked like he had just lost his lunch. "Joel!"

The suited man looked over while the younger guy turned and walked back toward the entrance to the building. "Knox, what are you doing here?"

Knox pointed a thumb back at Amber. "Amber called, said I should come down. What are you thinking this is?"

Joel shook his head. "Too soon to tell, really. Could just be some wacko trying to cash in. But…"

"But you don't think it is?" Knox asked.

Joel made eye contact with Amber and Lindsey, then looked back to Knox. He hesitated, then finally said, "No. The killer also opened the evidence box that had the masks from…your incident. All the masks were there, except one."

"The Host," Lindsey said, and Amber felt her

mother's grip tighten around her shoulders.

Joel nodded. "I know you're not a cop anymore, Knox, but I want to pull you in to consult. You two as well. I think this is just the beginning."

"Of what?" Amber asked

Joel looked at her. "A sequel."

CHAPTER 6

Knox sat in his office (the pathetic cubicle that it was) in the Academic Administration Building and tapped a pencil on his desk as the University President Holden Straub paced back and forth. He was worked up, angry and indignant that the Nacogdoches police had denied his request for more officers patrolling the campus.

"-like they don't care about the University's reputation at all!" he nearly shouted.

"Or the students who attend here, maybe?" Knox said quietly.

"What? Yeah, the students' safety is always paramount," Straub continued, barely registering Knox. "I mean, how do I convince our board of education that I have this under control? With my request for an increase in tuition, they want to make sure the money is being spent well and our University is safe- and now this!"

Knox sighed and leaned forward. "Dr. Straub, if I may?"

"I swear, if this hurts our ranking in any of those college recruitment polls, heads will roll! I mean, jobs will be at stake, Knox. Mine," he turned for the first time to fully recognize that Knox was there. "And of course, yours."

Gritting his teeth, Knox interjected, "I appreciate that situation, sir, but there are two things I should point out. One, the murder was not on- or near- campus. The police have no reason to suspect that King University is in danger. And two, I am your chief of security, and as such, I might have a bit more pull with the police when requesting more patrols. Plus, as I said, I am the chief of security, and will definitely be vigilant in those duties."

Straub seemed to consider this, then added, "Fine. No overtime though." Straub had never wanted to hire Knox, but the board had made it clear that to get Lindsey, they had to take Sully. Despite the wonders that did for Knox's pride, it did give his family a paycheck and a bit more financial security. Still, Straub consistently looked for ways to let Knox know he was unwanted.

"Wouldn't dream of it, sir," Knox said, leaning back in his chair. "But if I may ask- that new tuition hike- what's it for?"

Straub turned and faced Knox, his head glowing red beneath his thin gray hair, and the veins on his neck popping like some ridiculous cartoon. "That is none of your concern, Knox. Good day!" And he stormed out the door.

Knox rubbed his beard, which was mostly gray with some flecks of brown, and began to think. The police didn't have a reason to think King University was in trouble, but the fact was that someone claiming to be the Host was in Nacogdoches. And so was his family. Three of the four survivors of...what happened. "Crap," Knox said under his breath as he remembered there was one other person who probably needed to be kept in the loop. He pulled out his phone and dialed, then waited for an answer.

Before it came, he heard a ringtone outside his door- an old Hank Williams Jr song about how well suited for survival country boys were. Then in walked the man he had called- Claude Garvin. "Wondered when you'd git around to callin' me," he said.

"Claude, were you waiting out there?"

"Thought it'd make a grand entrance," he replied.

"How long were you waiting?" Knox asked.

"Jest as long as that red-faced fella was in there yellin' at ya," Claude answered. "He your boss?"

"Yeah," Knox said. "For now. He is not a fan, if you can't tell. So, you know about it? The murder?"

"Saw it on the news this mornin'" Claude said. "Hightailed it here, see how I can help."

Knox smiled in spite of himself. He had once found Claude to be an irritating and useless redneck. But then, during the incident in Kingston, he proved he was useful. Still an irritating redneck, but well intentioned and somewhat capable. His flirtation with fame of late had put some strain on their improving relationship, but deep down, Sully Knox had grown to like Claude Garvin. "I hope you can, but even I'm pretty sidelined on this. I'm not officially a cop anymore, even if the lead detective and I are friends, there is only so much I can do."

Claude's lips spread into a wide grin beneath his massive, bushy beard. "Well, it's a good thing I *am* a duly appointed officer of the law. Means I might be able ta get us a bit more info. Of course, I might need a deputy…" He cast a sly look at Knox. "Unpaid, of course."

Knox returned the smile. "Deal. Let's go." They stood up and walked out the door, headed for the police station.

◆ ◆ ◆

Amber was amazed at how quickly the small East Texas city had become ground zero for what seemed like every major news affiliate in the state. Maybe the nation.

Peacocks, eyes, letters in circles. Blue letters, red letters. Even some names that looked to be from different countries were lined up along the small roads snaking around King University's campus. Some students seemed intent on trying to catch a chance at a few moments of fame, but Amber kept her head down and kept walking.

As much as she was excited about Rogan's documentary, she felt a rising level of anxiety now that there had been a new murder. She doubted very much it had anything to do with her or her family, but Amber also knew that her family was inextricably linked to Killtown. And to any nut that wanted to copycat it by calling themselves the Host.

"Hey, you been interviewed yet?" Asher asked as he trotted up to Amber from the van with the big blue eye.

She pursed her lips and shrugged. "Not really trying to be, Asher. Saving my exclusive for Rogan's documentary."

"Fair enough," Asher replied, then cast a look over his shoulder. "They asked about you and your family, though. I played it cool, though."

She smiled kindly. "I appreciate that."

He looked around as if making sure no one was listening, then leaned closer to Amber. "We didn't get to talk last night. You think this murder is connected to...you know...like, for real?"

She shook her head. "I really don't. All of the killers are dead. Most of them were loners, no connections or even relatives that would want to make a go of a second Killtown. Their dark web site was found and shut down; they were the only contributors. I really think it's somebody trying to get famous in a horrific way. And they're a moron."

Asher grimaced and asked, "Moron? Why?"

"Why recycle a second-rate costumed murderer? It's not like you could pull off another Killtown," she started up the steps to the Liberal Arts building, where class was. "It's like Professor Newman says, 'copycats are too dumb to be original.'"

Ashton opened the door for Amber and said, "If it is a copycat."

Amber laughed mirthlessly. "They are all dead, Ashton. What else could it be?"

"Undead revenant?" he answered with a smile. "Either way, I don't think this is a pure copycat. I think it's a fan."

"Not of my podcast," Rogan said walking up to them as they crossed the lobby to the staircase leading to the second floor. "Heard what you guys were chatting about. I agree with Amber-"

"Naturally," Ashton said snarkily.

"-That it is a copycat. Why would they be a fan? I feel that between all the media coverage and my podcast any romance that might have existed about those guys has been dispelled."

"Unless it's a revenant," Amber said with a mischievous grin.

"Do you even know what a revenant is?" Ashton asked as they entered the hall outside the class.

"Like a zombie, right?" she replied.

Asher shook his head with mild disgust. It wasn't feigned, or even jokingly done- he took his horror seriously. "It is a corpse brought back to haunt the living. It isn't exactly mindless like a zombie. Think Jason. Some even think Michael Myers is one," he said with a grunt.

"Uh oh, you angered it," Rogan joked.

They entered a medium-sized lecture hall, seating about seventy-five. There were only about fifty people in the class, and the professor, Dr. Bennett Newman was a social teacher. He made it a point to get to know his students and often arrived early to chat with them informally. He was leaning back against the podium, his sandy-blonde hair neatly combed and his deep blue eyes looking out at Mikey, Liv, and Dex, who were the first to arrive. They were thirty minutes early, after all.

Amber's phone buzzed and she looked at her fitness tracker to see that a message from an unknown caller had said simply, "Hey- what's up?" Assuming it was a spam text, she ignored it.

"Oh, good," Dr. Newman said upon seeing them. "I'm glad you came in today, Amber. I wanted to chat with you- if that's alright?"

"Um, sure, Dr. Newman," she answered as she set her backpack down by Liv. "Everything okay?"

Newman put his arm around her shoulders gently and walked away from the group as he answered, "That's what I was going to ask you. I saw the news about last night, and I guess it might have hit a little close to home?"

Amber shrugged as she turned to face him. "A little. We were just talking about it. I really don't think it has anything to do with me or my parents, if that's what you mean."

Margot entered from the door behind the stage, and she seemed surprised to see everyone. Amber recalled that Newman's office was back there and she guessed Margot had been looking for him there. Newman paid her no attention. "I hope not, but I still think you need to be careful. Even if it is a copycat seeking fame- which I think it is- your family will always be connected to Killtown. Like it or not."

Amber rubbed her neck and looked at her feet. She knew that. She understood that. Yet, now that the murders might be starting up again, she decided she did not want to be that 'final girl' trope that all the horror movies had after all. It was fine to survive once, but if the killer kept coming back? The bad guy always coming for her until she is forced to kill him. Usually more than once. No, thank you. "I guess Nacogdoches isn't far enough from Kingston."

"No, Amber, twenty miles is not far enough for something like this," Newman said as he dropped his head to look at her face.

Her phone buzzed again. She checked her wrist. "What? Screening texts now?" the message from the unknown number read.

Ignored again.

Newman continued. "I won't bring it up in class today- but you should expect others to talk about it. I don't think they know who you are-outside of your group. But with this murder, that will probably change. Can you handle that?"

Amber looked at her friends. Rogan and Dex were joking around, Liv was reading something on her phone, and Asher was chatting with Margot- who kept cutting her eyes to look toward Amber and Newman. "I can. Look, professor, nobody outside of my friend group knows this, but I'm working with Rogan on getting his podcast turned into a documentary. I'm the star interview as well. It will be my first time talking to the media about it, and if they can keep that quiet, then I trust them to have my back if someone says something today. If it gets to be too much, I'll just step out."

The phone buzzed again. "Answer the text, please," the mystery messenger said. "Sorry, I need to respond to this," she said and stepped away from Newman. Amber pulled out her phone and looked at the messages. Other than the single lines, there was nothing else. She typed out, "I think you have the wrong number, sorry." Then she went to join her friends.

Newman followed behind her and when she walked up, Rogan looked at her and mouthed, "You okay?"

She nodded and took her seat next to Liv.

"Hey guys, I was just chatting with Amber," Newman said. "And since we are the only ones here for now, I wanted to give you the heads up. Expect talk about the murder last night. I will try to shut it down, for Amber's sake, but if any of you wanted to ask me now-" he raised his eyebrows as if indicating he was open.

Dex looked at Amber. "It's okay?"

She smiled and nodded.

Dex asked, "Do you think it's a copycat or a fan? See, Asher here thinks it's a murder fan. Rogan refuses to accept his podcast could inspire such a thing," he said with some good-natured snark. Rogan punched him playfully. "I guess what I'm asking is, as a criminology professor, what do you think this guy is all about?"

Newman smiled, then leaned back against the desk again, crossing his arms. "Well, Dex, there has been only one murder. Hard to say much. And there is so little information available right now. It could be either a fan or copycat."

"To be fair, I also threw out revenant," Asher chimed in.

Newman chuckled. "It's not a revenant. They aren't real, Ashton."

"What do you know, you're just a criminologist," Ashton joked. "Not a cryptozoologist."

They all laughed.

Then Margot asked, "What about a survivor?"

The room grew quiet as every eye turned to her.

Rogan looked confused. "A survivor? Like Amber and her family?"

Margot shrugged. "There was that other

guy, too. Claude- didn't you just interview him yesterday?" Rogan nodded. "Trauma does strange things. Then there was that cop- the one that killed the last guy. That had to mess with him. No one has heard much from him since that whole thing went down. I think he avoided the media like Amber did." She said the last little bit with a twinge of bitterness.

For the first time, Liv spoke up, turning to Margot. "What's that supposed to mean? You suggesting Amber was involved?"

"No, not at all," Margot said, putting her hands up defensively. "But didn't Patty Hearst get that...what's it called...Stockholm Syndrome from her captors? She started robbing banks after that."

"Amber wasn't kidnapped," Liv said, her voice firm. "She was nearly murdered. She was only with that clown guy for what, a few hours? Right Amber?"

"Yeah," Amber answered. "But psychologists think it doesn't take long for Stockholm to set in. Not that I'm saying I had it, by any means. Look, Margot, I was with you when they found the body, so I know you don't think I did it. Besides- that guy had to weigh two hundred pounds. You think I could lift him?"

"You were a cheerleader. Didn't you lift other people in pyramids or whatever?" Asher asked.

Amber looked at him with a smirk. "I was a flyer, thank you very much. They lifted me. And stringing up dead weight is not like lifting another athlete, anyway."

"Yeah, Asher knows nothing about athletics," Mikey said and they all laughed. Except Asher.

The doors to the back of the classroom opened and students started to file in, so the conversation shifted. Amber felt the buzz once more, and looked at her wrist. "No, this is the right number. I'm sure of it." Amber texted back. "Who are you looking for?" Then turned to Liv. "Thank you," she said. "Not sure what's bothering Margot. But I kinda felt attacked."

Liv raised her eyebrows. "You haven't heard? Rumors going around she and Dr. Newman are a thing. And there's other rumors, too."

Always up for some gossip, Amber got excited. "Oh, what is that pray tell?"

Liv looked around and leaned in close. "Dr. Benny has a thing for students. Margot isn't the first. And if I'm being honest, I saw the way he looked at you. You better watch yourself, girl!"

Amber laughed and looked back at Dr. Newman who was greeting other students. Then she glanced at Rogan, who looked up and smiled at her. She felt her cheeks blush and turned back Liv. "Not interested."

"I bet you aren't," Liv replied knowingly.

Buzz. "I'm looking for you, Amber." She felt her pulse race. Something felt very wrong. All of a sudden, all of her good humor and calm demeanor vanished. "Who is this?" she asked in the text.

"Alright class. Let's get started," Newman began class by taking roll, but Amber was watching her phone, waiting for a response. She tapped her foot rapidly, and did her best to hide her face from any prying eyes.

"Today we are going to talk about victimology, or the study of victims in crimes," Dr. Crewe was explaining. "See, rarely are crimes purely random. Even a basic mugging will see the criminal target certain people. The elderly, the person with a disability, a person on their phone that's distracted," he said this with a wink to hint it was time to put the phone up.

Amber looked away from the phone, then put it away. There had been no response.

"See, criminals are profilers," Newman continued. "They look for victims they can easily control. Burglars are known to be less likely to break into houses with dogs or houses near street lights. Those victims are not as attractive as the victims in a dark, quiet cul-de-sac where there is less traffic."

"Professor?" asked a voice in the back. "What is the victimology of killing a cop at an evidence locker? He wouldn't be an easy target, would he?"

"Listen, we are not going to talk about the murder last night," Newman said casually. "There just isn't enough information to speak intelligently about it."

"Okay, but if you had to guess?" the questioner prodded.

Newman glanced at Amber, who nodded that it was okay.

"Well, with zero information, my guess would be that the cop might have been collateral damage," Newman said. "Wrong place, wrong time."

"But why the public display?" the questioner continued. "Why not just leave the body inside without a message? Didn't the killer risk a lot to hang the body and write the message?"

"That...would imply- and again, this is just conjecture- that...there will be more victims," Newman said to a silent room.

Buzz. "Don't pretend you don't know me," said the message on Amber's wrist. There was a spinning wheel, indicating that an attachment was coming.

"Now, let's get back on topic. Victimology in more serious crimes of a random nature has a lot to do with psychology. A criminal will target certain people for physical similarities to their real target. Or perhaps behavioral similarities. They have a type, as it were. And then, there are those criminals who like to victimize their targets again and again.

Buzz. Amber pulled her phone out and stifled a scream.

It was the mask of Mr. Blue.

She shot out of her seat and sent her

notebook flying. Heads turned to follow her, and Rogan rose to follow her, waving the rest of the group off.

She ran into the hall outside and fell to the floor, tears running down her face. Rogan burst through the door and turned his head up and down the hall, looking for her. When he saw her, he knelt down next to her and asked, "What happened?"

She showed him the texts, and he said simply, "We need to call your parents."

Amber nodded, and taking Rogan's hand, she stood up.

Then her eyes fell on the bulletin board across the hall from the classroom entrance.

There were at least twenty pictures of a Mr. Blue mask scattered around the board.

And in the center was a picture of the wooden mask of the Host.

CHAPTER 7

The police station was buzzing with activity, but Knox and Claude found Detective Joel easily. He was at the back of the room, surrounded by uniformed officers and pointing at a cork board filled with evidence photos.

"The killer knew what he was going for, went right to the Kingston Mass Murder box," Joel said, pointing a picture of the evidence box sitting on the table. "No other box was disturbed. And aside from removing the other masks to get to the 'Host' mask, nothing else was taken from the box. We think that means the perpetrator is intending to commit more crimes, using said mask."

One uniformed officer raised his hand and asked, "If he wants to recreate Killtown, why not take all the masks?"

"Because if he wants to recreate Killtown, he has to invite new killers in. Even if they take on the same personas, there has to be an invitation," said a plainclothes detective sitting in the front by Joel. Knox assumed it was the new partner, the one who got sick at the scene the night before. The young man looked familiar, but his face was marked with scars- a feature that would have been cemented in Knox's memory. He turned his attention to the rundown of the case instead of chasing that rabbit.

"Detective Faust is a sort of expert on this case," Joel said, indicating the man who had just spoken. "You may recognize him as the man who took down Sean Densman. Nickname, 'The Novice.' Densman escaped the mill, but was killed in a gunfight with then Officer Faust, on his first day, right?"

Faust turned to look at the crowd for the first time, and Knox felt his heart skip a beat. Getting a good look at the young detective for the first time, he saw what it was about the man. Knox was floored with the similarity between the cop and the kid who had shed blood in his town. He had seen side-by-side pictures on the news and knew there was a resemblance but seeing him face-to-face was an entirely different experience.

Detective Faust and Sean Densman could have been brothers.

"Yeah, heck of an introduction," Faust said sheepishly. Then he saw Knox and Claude standing at the back of the room and said, "Hey, Joel, I'm not the only expert here today."

Detective Joel waved Knox and Claude over. "Everyone, this is retired Police Chief of Kingston, Sullivan Knox and current Chief Claude Garvin. They were survivors of the Kingston murders."

The officers turned and looked, some with

awe, others with disinterest. While Claude beamed, Knox felt a strong urge to hide. He hated attention being drawn to himself about what happened in Kingston. He was called survivor and hero, but he only felt like one thing.

A failure.

Then, he wondered to himself, why had he come to the police station? He knew he would have all those stares, but he came anyway. Part of Sullivan Knox, a part he could never share with anyone else, not even Lindsay, wanted the killer to be back. Because it meant a chance at redemption.

Joel continued. "These two men are going to be aiding us in this investigation. Now, I have not formally invited them, but I will remedy that right now. Gentlemen, welcome to our task force."

Claude had a grin from ear to ear, but Knox merely nodded.

"Feel free to interject whenever, guys," Joel said, then turned back to the board. "So, as of right now, this is just a singular crime. Even if we expect more, we treat this as a one-off. The preliminary results of Officer Volker's autopsy show that two knives were used. Similar blades, but slightly different in size. Based on what we know, that differs from Kingston, right?"

"Yep, none of them used more than one blade, 'cept the big fella," Claude said. "But them weapons were chainsaws and machetes and axes."

Knox was still looking at Faust. He couldn't get over the similarities. What were the odds that two men so near in appearance would find themselves face-to-face, let alone in a fight to the death? But then, since the murder spree, Knox had come to believe that the irrationally impossible happened far more often than he'd care to see.

"Right, so is this simply an imitation or an escalation?" Joel asked.

"I've studied the Killtown event extensively," Faust said. "And it is important to note that the podcast from our own King University has become something of a viral sensation. Add to the intense media coverage in the year after the event, and you have a population well-versed in the crimes. I think this is an imitation, yes. But I also think the two knives might be a declaration that this Host plans to ramp up the stakes."

A female officer asked, "So, will there be some sort of invitation? Like the first time? Will more killers come?"

"We need to prepare for that," Joel said. "We are looking at increasing police presence in and around both colleges here in Nacogdoches, and King University in particular, which is another reason I'm glad to see Knox here. We will be ready for whatever comes at us."

"No, you won't," Knox said to himself. Unfortunately, he said it loud enough for everyone to hear.

Joel looked at Knox, and asked, "Why do you say that?"

Sighing, Knox looked around sheepishly. "Well, if this guy is trying to recreate Kingston, then he intends to bring chaos. All the shows and even that podcast talk about Mr. Blue- that clown- as the one who brought the chaos. But he was just a tool. The Host, he- or they- are the instrument of true chaos. Think about it, who invites sadistic murderers to take part in a sick game? Someone who wants to terrorize and tear down society. The clown wanted to attack institutions, but the Host was more personal. They wanted to get their petty vengeances under the cover of it being something more. If this person is trying to be the new Host, don't just look at the obvious. What you see clearly is probably just a front for something far more personal."

Faust looked at Knox and asked, "So, was Volker personal, then?"

Knox shrugged. "Don't know. But probably not. I think he was just in the wrong place at the wrong time. But maybe he's the key to it all. Or maybe, the killer is just making it up as they go along."

As if fate wanted to discredit Knox, his phone began to buzz. As did Joel's and Faust's. Knox looked down at the screen and felt his stomach drop. The text from Lindsey read:

"Get to campus now. He sent Amber a message."

◆ ◆ ◆

Lindsey sat with her arm around Amber, who was taking deep breaths and getting her tears under control. She was rubbing her daughter's back and trying to get her to answer the officer's questions when Holden Straub burst into Dr. Newman's office, where they had set up.

"What is going on here? Where is my chief of security?" Straub demanded. "There are at least two dozen camera crews outside this building unspooling all sorts of nefarious yarns about my university and not one person can tell me what is happening."

Lindsey looked up at Straub and calmly- but firmly- replied, "My daughter was sent text messages with veiled threats relating to the murder last night, as well as our shared traumatic experience. Now, please keep your voice down."

Straub huffed, then grimaced at Lindsey, "I will remind myself that you are being a parent right now, and not my employee, and forgive your tone. Is there a danger to my campus? And where is your husband?"

"Right here," Knox said, entering the room and rushing to Amber. He was followed by two detectives- Joshua Joel who she recognized and one she did not- and bringing up the rear was Claude Garvin. "Amber, are you hurt? Did someone come after you?"

"J-just messages," Amber managed. "On my phone. But on th-the b-bulletin board outside the class- there were pictures..."

Joel nodded to his young partner, who left to go examine the board.

"What kind of pictures?" Joel asked, pointing for the officer who had been asking questions to go help the detective.

"Mostly of the clown, from K-kingston," she said. "But also of the Host."

"Amber, Detective Joel will need your phone, to see if he can trace the messages," Knox said. "Can he have it?"

Lindsey had it in her hand, and she quickly passed it to Detective Joel. Then she asked, "Is Amber in danger? Do we need to, what, get protective custody?"

"That's up to you folks," Joel said, looking to Knox. "Ordinarily, I would recommend it, but with Knox here, you kind of have that already built in."

"No offense, Sully, but can we please have at least some officers watching the house?" Lindsey said, trying to soften the blow to her husband's ego as much as she could.

To her surprise, he agreed readily. "Whatever you need to feel safe. Amber, it goes without saying that you are staying with us for the time being."

"Excuse me, but wouldn't that send a message to the other students that it is not safe to stay in our dorms?" Straub asked. "If our chief of security thinks his home is safer than our campus?"

"Well, now, Holden, I think it would point out that I am being a good father and taking care of my daughter, who is in the unique position of being one of only four survivors of the event this nut is copying. And that she was *directly* messaged by someone claiming to be a killer. And if you worry the students feel unsafe all of a sudden, maybe send some of that tuition increase you keep talking to more cameras on campus and more security lights, rather than into your own bank account," Knox said sarcastically.

Once again, Straub's face turned red and he began to repeat what he had said to Lindsey, "I will remind myself that you are being a parent right now-"

"I would not finish that sentence, Holden," Lindsey interrupted. "Because if you do and my husband doesn't punch you in the mouth, I will."

Straub's jaw dropped open and he stormed out of the room, past Detective Joel who was barely suppressing a laugh.

"Would you have arrested me if I did, Joshua?" Lindsey asked.

"I'd be more inclined to arrest you if you didn't," the detective replied.

◆ ◆ ◆

Faust was taking pictures of the bulletin board when Straub stomped down the stairs and made a beeline for the media gathered just outside the doors. He was mumbling something about 'insubordination.'

The initial shock of having seen the masks of Killtown spilled out on the table the night before and the Host mask being absent had faded. But the picture of those haunting red eyes glaring back at Cade made him shiver. He saw flashes, time and again of that mask from three years before. Lunging at him, attacking him. The struggle to survive in the mud and the muck of the lakeside as the two men battled for the weapon.

Cade had survived that day, and as part of his own personal therapy, he had studied Killtown. He watched every true crime show on the networks and cable. He listened to Rogan Benson's podcast. And he had studied case files. In his interview to become a detective, he talked a lot about how his trauma had made him a better profiler, a better detective. That his first case as a detective would be in direct response to his first call as an officer and that it would be about *that* case- it was as if fate had decided Killtown was his destiny.

He wondered if the Knox family felt that way. That Killtown chased them wherever they went. Cade had researched them, too, and it seemed that they had moved on. Lindsey Knox wrote the book on Killtown, and of course, Cade had read it. He could tell she was using it at therapy, and he could relate. His ordeal had been minutes, hers had been hours, but she captured the confusion that often fogged reality when one survived such a horrific experience.

The door opened again, and Cade heard Holden Straub speaking to the media. He was telling them that King University was safe, that students could rest securely, knowing that the killer would never set foot on the campus.

Cade knew that was a bold promise, and one that the university president could not hope to keep. Not that they wouldn't do everything they could to keep the campus safe, but the man had just painted a target on his campus' back. As Cade looked on, he saw someone moving behind the crowd of reporters. They were clad in dark clothes, and he couldn't make out a face. "Keep taking photos, I need to check something," he told the officer with him, then he moved toward the doors.

As he did, he texted Joel that he thought he might see the suspect- or someone suspicious, anyway- at the press conference. Joel replied that he would send some officers down as well.

Cade moved past the media as Straub talked about "- unprecedented levels of coordination between campus security and local law enforcement to ensure that no blood was spilled on King University campus." Cade hoped that was true.

The figure had begun to move away slowly and by the time Cade got to the back of the crowd, they were gone. He clicked his phone into walkie mode and rang Joel. "Lost sight of him, he's on the move." Then, a flutter of movement came around the corner of the building. "He's moving around the building opposite the crime scene," Cade said quietly into the phone, then he drew his weapon and advanced cautiously. He was discreet and no one saw him moving, the uniforms were starting to emerge from the sides of the building and were moving to secure the scene when Cade reached the corner of the building. He took a deep breath and cleared the corner.

And felt a hot slash of pain and fire across his arm. He fired the gun once, then all went black.

Seconds later, he opened his eyes and looked around the small alley.

It was empty.

Two uniformed officers ran up behind him just then- but the suspect had disappeared. Blood was running down his arm and laying at his feet was a hunting knife, a dark red liquid along the edge of the blade.

So much for Straub's promise of 'no bloodshed' on King University's campus.

The killer had been there, after all. But was long gone.

And once more, Cade Faust had gotten very lucky.

◆ ◆ ◆

"Okay, now we definitely need armed protection," Lindsey said to Knox as they watched an EMT stitch up Cade Faust's arm. Amber stood between them, her tears gone but now a dark weariness settling into her eyes.

"Agreed," Knox said.

Lindsey didn't like what she was seeing. Someone was coming for her family again. Cops could say it was coincidence or that there wasn't enough proof that they were a target yet, but Lindsey knew. A mother always knew when her kids were in danger. She watched as an officer bagged a hunting knife, one not all that different from the ones used in Killtown. She felt certain it was starting again. Different, yet more of the same.

At that moment, a siren blared. It was the storm warning siren for the campus. It's a long, bellowing sound that folks in Tornado Alley are all too familiar with. But the sky was a deep cerulean blue without a cloud to be seen.

Then came the voice.

"People of King University, your president has promised you protection. He is a thief and a liar. Blood will be shed here before the sun rises, and you will see that he has deceived you. I am the Host, and this- this is just the beginning."

The horn blared again, and then screams and yells filled the air.

"Look," Amber said, pointing to the electric

marquee that ran announcements in front of the student center, just across the way from where they were standing.

Normally, it featured announcements about games or events cycling through and ending on the phrase "Welcome to King U!"

At that moment, it read: "Welcome to Kill U!"

KILLTOWN: SEASON 2, EPISODE 2

If the cliche "all good things must come to an end" is true, does that mean that evil never dies?

Welcome to a special, live podcast of Killtown, as we have breaking news about what might just be the continuation of the story we have been telling.

Over the last twenty-four hours, Nacogdoches has learned that perhaps evil does live forever. Last night, Officer Charles Volker, a veteran officer, was killed while performing his duty at the evidence warehouse for NPD. As tragic as this is, what is horrifying is how he was discovered, and what he may have been killed for.

Some of what follows is fact- gleaned from various news sources and some inside tips. Some is an educated guess on my part.

Fact: Charlie Volker was stabbed to death,

and then his body was hung from the front of the evidence warehouse complete with a message.

"I'm back- The Host."

I saw these things with my own eyes. When I began the Killtown Podcast, I never imagined that I might see such horror for myself. The message was written in blood- BLOOD! And he was displayed for the entire town to see. And many did, judging from the size of the crowd that rushed to the scene last night.

Educated guess: The public display of Officer Volker was a message. Obviously, one was written in blood. But the message was not simply about claiming to be the Host from Killtown, it was about declaring that there would be more death to come. Obviously, I do not believe this is the Host from Killtown. Jane Sharp and Nate Clupe died that night almost three years ago. This is definitive. It is also true for all of the other murderers that night- all are dead as doornails. Also, this new killer is not- as a friend of my jokingly suggested- a revenant. Some undead or reanimated form of the killers. At least, I hope he was joking. No, I believe that someone killed Officer Volker and claimed to be the Host because they want to lay claim to the fame surrounding Killtown.

Fact: Something was taken from evidence.

Educated guess: That something was related to Killtown. Perhaps a weapon, but I suspect it was one of the Host masks. We know there were two, and that one had been taken by Sean Densman. It is well known that he was wearing it when he was killed by the officer we now know to be Cade Faust- more on him soon. I suspect the authentic Host mask was the reason for the break-in.

Fact: Now, this is where I share new information- information that no media source has shared yet. Information that again, I saw first hand. One of the original survivors of Killtown- who I will not name- was targeted by someone claiming to be Mr. Blue. Mr. Blue, the clown killer. He messaged the survivor and left a veiled threat that he was watching them. He also peppered pictures of the Mr. Blue mask along with the Host mask near this survivor.

Educated guess: The killer will be targeting survivors of Killtown. I have, as you regular listeners know, come to know all of them fairly well, with the exception of newly minted Detective Cade Faust. It terrifies me- and I am sure, them- that some sick, depraved individual would target these people for no other reason than to 'finish what was started.' While the killer will be targeting these people, I also believe that there will be more targets. As to the Mr. Blue who made the call- I think it is the same person who killed Officer Volker. But- and this is a big 'but-' it is possible that the new Host is actually trying to recreate Killtown. I believe he may be inviting killers to Nacogdoches- and specifically to King University.

Fact: Digital messaging at King University was hijacked today by someone claiming to be the Host.

Educated guess: I think the new Host has targeted the University because of this podcast. No- I do not think it is all about me. I think the killer believes they can use this podcast to gain fame. Notoriety.

That being said, I realize that even this small discussion of the matter will bring attention to the vile person who is seeking it. So, I will be suspending the Killtown podcast until the killer is apprehended. I will not give this monster a second of attention if it means they will be inspired to kill more people.

So, for the time being, this is Rogan Benson, signing off.

CHAPTER 8

"I am so glad you had that boy stop doing that horrid podcast," Nikki Meyers said smugly as she sat in Holden Straub's office as the last rays of the fall sun beamed through the window. She was accompanied by her apparent sidekick, Reverend Felix Casey. The large man with the slicked back hair, goatee, and crazy eyes was nodding in agreement and muttering "Amen" to all she said.

"I didn't make him," Straub clarified. "He chose to do it on his own." Then, realizing he admitted a minor lapse of his control, he added, "But I was going to suggest it, anyway."

"Well, President Straub, as you know, my husband and I are *strong* financial supporters of King University," Nikki said condescendingly. "We would have hated to pull our donations over such a...trivial thing. But we must do what we know is right in our hearts and the Lord's eyes. Don't you agree, Reverend?"

Casey nodded again, and with his usual blustery overcompensation, said, "Sister Meyers speaks sound truth. And our Church does wield considerable influence in the community." The veiled threat was not so veiled. Or accurate. Casey's church was little more than a collection of extremists.

Straub nodded anyway. He was a modestly religious man himself, but Nikki Meyers and Felix Casey were the sort of Christians that wielded their faith like a cudgel. If they didn't like something, their Jesus must not like it either. And He would gladly pummel it into oblivion or empower Nikki Meyers and Felix Casey to dismantle the offensive thing.

Nikki and the Reverend rose and turned to leave, then stopped. She turned once more and said, "Now that the podcast is gone, we will need to talk about this-ugh- pro-choice club that has started having meetings on campus," she glared down her nose at Straub, and even though he was the figure in power, he demurred.

"Of course, Mrs. Meyers," Straub said obediently. "Whatever we need to do to make sure you feel good about your donations going to a good cause." Making sure Casey wasn't watching, he winked at Nikki. It was not an innocent gesture.

She smiled a saccharinely sweet smile- that was wholly disingenuous- and left.

Casey turned back and pointed at Straub while making a motion as if to indicate he was praying for him. Straub assumed said prayer was less about protecting and loving him than it was about repentance.

Straub waited a moment to make sure they

were gone, then he opened the bottom drawer of his desk and pulled out a bottle of whiskey and a glass. Couldn't have the temperance minded Nikki Meyers knowing about his little bit of liquid stress relief. Even if she was a willing participant in some of his...other stress relief.

And there was a lot of stress for the president. The new tuition hike was about to go into effect, and it couldn't happen sooner. Straub needed a raise, and fast. He remembered a time when he had gotten into education to make a difference, but time and finances wore him down. Once he achieved administration, it became less about education and more about securing and advancing his own status and wealth.

But he had made some bad financial calls of late, and he owed some money. Plus, the economy was rife with inflation, and even Straub's six figure salary wasn't cutting it.

He took a sip of the whiskey, then followed with another in rapid succession.

His mind turned to the murder of the cop, and the threats on his campus. For good measure, he downed the rest of the glass. He lifted the bottle and poured another.

He heard a cackle from outside his window and turned to see that it was just Nikki Meyers, talking loudly on her cell phone via her earpiece. Straub was unsettled, that was certain. A killer on a college campus was a terrible thing, and to Straub that was no more clearly evident than where it related to the risk to the bottom line of King University's finances.

Straub's gaze followed Meyers as she walked beneath the streetlamps and disappeared beneath the canopy of pine trees. Nikki was a pain for sure, but Straub was envious of her commitment to an ideal. Even if she was a raging hypocrite. He and Nikki had been engaging in an affair for a little over a year, and she seemed unperturbed by the idea that she railed against immorality while she herself was pretty immoral. Especially after dark.

She was passionate (in more ways than one), whereas far too often Straub felt like a mere cog in the big system. And a cog that was far too underpaid in its own estimation.

He turned from the window and just missed a dark shape rush from the darkness into the front door of the building.

Holden Straub surveyed his kingdom- that was how he saw the campus. And like a king of old, he felt entitled to a regal paycheck. It was true that the tuition hikes were mostly going to pad his paycheck, but then, King University was doing *very* well in his tenure.

Attendance was up, there had been some amazing hires come aboard the faculty, and the campus was a beautiful gem to the city of Nacogdoches.

He would never admit it to Sullivan Knox, but with the hoopla surrounding the possible copycat running around, the thought of hiring extra security had crossed his mind. However, the budget was tight.

Tightly held in Holden Straub's hands.

He had grown accustomed to nice things. Straub had been a lower administrator at a much larger state college but had taken the job at King a few years earlier because it paid well. When the economy tanked following the pandemic, and then inflation set in, he found the finer things in life to be just out of reach.

So, he had begun to…redirect money.

He fired the financial manager and placed himself in charge, which made sense because he had been a finance professor in his teaching days. So, there were no questions. And as long as the university kept raking in money, no one looked too closely at a few thousand here and there.

But the new tuition hike was needed because Holden Straub had begun to outspend his ability to quietly cook the books. Even big funders like Nikki Meyers couldn't give enough to help. Which reminded Holden. He picked up the phone and dialed a familiar number.

"Saul, it's Holden," he said when the voice of his college friend answered. "Yes, I did get your email, that was why I called. Sorry to bother you so late, but I am sure you have heard the news…yes, yes, it is bad…No, I think the local authorities have it under control for now…No, Saul, I don't need you throwing your congressman weight around on this. But I do need some help…

Yes, that donation you mentioned, any chance you could speed up the timetable? Next week would be great...yeah, I appreciate that...Looking forward to it." Then he hung up and took a deep breath. That donation would buy him some time. He set the whiskey glass down on the desk and rubbed his face. Then he heard a shuffling sound outside. "Pietro- that you?" Pietro was the cleaning man that worked the night shift. There was no response.

His desk phone rang, and when he looked he saw it was the intercom from his secretary's desk. He was drunk enough to push the button. "Yvette? That you?" He knew it wasn't.

But the voice that answered still sent shivers down his back. "You know this isn't Yvette, Holden Straub," came the mechanical and hollow sounding voice. "Just like you know that what you've been up to is evil. Bad. Dishonest. And that you need to pay up."

"I'm calling the police," Holden said and hung up the intercom. When he tried to dial 9-11 out, there was only static. He grabbed his cell and called the number. "Yes, this is Holden Straub and I am in my office at the University. I think there is someone here that shouldn't be."

"This is King University?" the operator asked, their voice a male baritone.

"Yes," Holden replied.

"Ah, yes. I see," the operator confirmed. "I see that there is someone there that shouldn't be."

Suddenly, there was a click, and the mechanized voice was on the other end of the line. "You."

A dark shape moved into the doorway and Holden Straub froze.

A tattered black cape was draped over the shoulders of the figure, and there were strands of black cloth wrapped around black gloved wrists and around their thigh. There was a large black hunting knife in one hand and a silver blade in the other. A black hood surrounded a wooden mask, the grain of the wood black against a reddish-tan stain. A saw blade smile was flashing at him beneath twin red, circular eyes that glinted in the light. One had cracks in it, and surrounding that eye was powderburn and what looked to be buckshot. As Holden stared for what seemed to be an eternity, he saw that the entire mask was pockmarked with tiny bullet holes.

The figure stepped forward, and as it moved, it spoke. "You are a thief and a philanderer, Holden Straub. One that evades the law at every turn because no one suspects. But your deeds do not escape the eyes of the Host. For we are the Host, and we are all-knowing."

"I-I'll give you whatever you want, just let me go," Holden said, stepping back from his desk as the Host advanced.

"I doubt that you would. Or that you could," the Host said, moving forward, the knives spinning in their hands. "But you will have the honor of being the inaugural kill of the new

Killtown. Every Killtown has to have a first sacrifice- a victim that shocks everyone and at the same time hints at what is to come- and why that doom is to come. It's oh so appropriate that I will begin teaching the lessons of Kill U with the president of the college."

The Host took a breath, and Holden moved forward to his desk and placed one hand on top. With his other hand, he opened a drawer on his desk. "Look, I keep some cash here, j-just in case. You can have it all-"

With blinding speed, the silver blade in the Host's left hand came down on Holden's hand on the desk. Rather, it went through his hand. Straub screamed in pain and dropped to his knees. The second knife slashed across his face and tore open a gash of flesh across his cheek. The Host pulled the first knife free, then spun it in its hand and drove the blade into Holden's chest. The Host did the same with the other knife, and then lifted Holden up against his window. "P-please...no..." Holden managed, but then the Host began to rapidly remove and restab each knife, counting out the wounds as they went.

"Twenty-three, twenty-four, twenty-five," the Host monotonously continued. Holden began to gurgle blood as the punctures kept coming. He felt the blades of the first two dozen stabs with startling clarity. He felt one puncture his lung, another must have snagged on an intestine, and it was torn out of his body. After that, he just felt the pressure and the force of the blows, nothing else.

Finally, the Host stopped at, "Fifty-two." They grabbed the handles of both knives, placed a foot on Holden Straub's chest, and kicked. His body flew through the window and fell three stories to the ground below. A pool of blood quickly began to spread, and the Host turned back to the desk. The opened drawer had several files in it, and the Host rifled through them until they found what they wanted. Then they raced down the stairs.

Straub's body was still twitching when the Host got to it, and they knelt beside him. The Host placed a file on Holden's chest, reached around behind their back and pulled a third, smaller knife out and jabbed it through the file into Straub's chest.

"Hey- what are you doing over there?" called out a male voice from the dark.

The Host lifted his head and saw a college man walking into the light. He was about ten feet away when the Host rose to his feet and unsheathed his knives. "Wrong place, wrong time."

Realization spread across the college guy's face, but the Host moved quicker than the kid's brain. The gap between them was closed with lightning speed. The black blade slashed the young man's throat, the second sliced open his gut. The boy's body fell not ten feet from Holden Straub, then the Host took the knives and sheathed them. He wanted to work quickly, in case someone did happen to show up to investigate. Then the Host stuck a gloved finger in the blood and began to write on the cement above Holden Straub's head.

❖ ❖ ❖

At some point in the middle of the night, Rogan awoke to the sound of movement in his bedroom. He raised up on one elbow and rubbed his eyes with the other hand. As his vision began to clear, he saw a dark shape standing near the foot of his bed.

"Holy sh-" he began to exclaim before the figure raised a gloved finger in a shushing motion to the mouth of the wooden mask with red eyes.

"You will continue to tell my story on your podcast, Rogan," the mechanized voice said. "Or I will visit you again. Then I will be much more... convincing."

"Wh-who are you?" Rogan managed.

The head tilted and the voice replied, "Why, the Host of course. And see, I also know of your little documentary deal. Keep doing the podcast, and not only will I let you live, I'll make you famous."

"What do you mean?" Rogan said, pulling his feet up as close as he could to his body.

"I mean, an exclusive. With me. All about

the Host and my evil plans."

Rogan pondered. He was going to say whatever he needed to in order to survive the encounter, but the entrepreneur in him thought the deal sounded good. Too good, maybe. "Why are you doing this? Why me?"

The head tilted once more. "Fair enough, here is a little taste of my motive. I am not a villain- I am a product of the true villains. Those who create systems that enslave, subjugate, and crush those just trying to survive in it. I chose you because…well, you always gave me a fair shake in your podcasts."

"B-but you died," Rogan said. "All of the killers in Killtown are dead. You're a copycat- you can't be the original Host."

The Host sighed. "Well, I guess we shall see who I really am together, now won't we?" The Host backed away and faded into the shadows of the room.

Rogan jumped out of bed and ran to see where the figure had gone. The hall outside his apartment was empty, but his front door stood wide open.

His knees gave out, and he sank to the floor.

CHAPTER 9

"Follow the money."

Cade read the message out loud as he stared down at the bloody mess that had been Holden Straub.

The first rays of the sun were starting to peek over the top of the dome of the Academic Administration office, but the most abundant source of light came from the blue and red flashing lights surrounding the building. Once again, Cade was bathed in their hues.

A few feet to his right was the body of a college senior, identified as Ray Oswald. And Cade had no idea why that kid was there.

"This isn't his style," Knox was saying as he sipped a coffee and stood with Detective Joel and Claude. "The Host wasn't the riddle leaving kind. That was more the Clown. Mr. Blue. And do you know what it means? The message?"

Joel leaned down and looked at the papers stabbed into Straub's chest. "These look like financial documents, but I'll need to examine them more closely. Doc, any idea on cause of death?"

The medical examiner was across from Joel

and looked up. Drily, he said, "The fifty-three stab wounds and three story fall probably had something to do with it." Joel glared. "Which is to say, I'll know for sure when I do the full autopsy."

"Fifty-three stab wounds?" Claude said with a whistle and a curse. "Dontcha boys call that 'overkill' or somethin' like that?"

"Overkill or a message," Cade said as he took a photo of Oswald's body.

Knox looked over at him. Cade knew that his appearance- looking so much like Sean Densman- weirded Knox out. Heck, sometimes it weirded Cade out. But he wanted to win Knox over. The dude was still a good cop, and Cade was certain they needed him working with them. So, Cade explained, "'Follow the Money' and some financial statements stabbed into the vic tell me the killer thinks Straub had financial secrets worth killing for. Maybe the fifty-three stab wounds are part of *that* message."

Knox rubbed his chin. Then asked, "How soon can we get a look at those papers?"

The M.E. shrugged. "Now. I need to move them before I move him."

Joel nodded, and then the M.E. removed the knife from the dead man's chest and dropped it into an evidence baggie. Joel produced a larger bag and put the papers in it. "Can we go to your office, Knox?"

Claude laughed. "If ya c'n call it that."

"Shut up, Claude," Knox said back, smiling at

Cade. "He wouldn't be a cop if it weren't for me," he said to Cade.

"I wouldn't be here period, if it weren't fer you," Claude retorted. Cade wasn't sure if Claude meant that as a compliment or a curse.

❖ ❖ ❖

"I'm glad you all came," Rogan said as he looked around the recording booth at all of those present.

Amber had gotten the call from Rogan at four in the morning, a frantic and terrified tone from her friend brought her out of a dead sleep. She assumed that Dex, Liv, Asher, Margot, and Mikey had gotten a similarly breathless call, as they were all sitting around her at that moment, waiting for Rogan to explain.

Rogan paced back and forth, rubbing his hands together and mumbling to himself. Dex broke the tension by asking, "Dude, you having a breakdown or something?"

Rogan laughed nervously and said, "*And* something. Um, look. There is no easy way to say this, so I'll just say it. The Host came to my bedroom last night."

"Was it a dirty dream?" Asher quipped.

Rogan glared at him with an intensity that shifted the mood instantly. "A freakin' murderer stood over my bed last night. I'm not up for the jokes, Asher."

Asher made a face and replied, "Sorry, man. But...why are you still alive if he came to visit?"

Rogan looked at Amber and she thought she saw regret in his eyes. Then he explained, "He wants me to keep doing the podcast. Says he thinks I've treated him well so far."

"Wait," Amber said, holding up her hand. "What does that mean? The Host from...my situation...they're dead. Jane Sharp and Nate Clute are dead. *Dead* dead. I saw it with my own eyes. Kinda helped make it happen."

"Okay, any chance one of the other killers survived?" Mikey asked.

Amber shook her head. "The Pyro died in the street after getting hit by a firetruck. The Wraith was impaled on a fence at the church after Pastor Bob tossed him out a window. The big one, the Brute, he was...sawed and shot by my dad. And the clown...Sean Densman's body crushed him to death. The kid, Sean, got away for a bit. But then a cop killed him."

"Wait," Margot said, raising a hand. "Wasn't there another guy? A guy who was supposed to be a good guy, even though he was a killer? Tommy?"

Rogan nodded. "Yeah, but he died in the lake. From a booby trap the Host had set up. But guys, finding out the Host's identity is not a priority for me right now. What do I do about the killer demanding I keep recording?"

"Ok, you keep recording. Keep telling the

story," Mikey said. "It seems that will keep you safe."

"Which is convenient," Asher said. Everyone looked at him.

"What? It's victimology, right? Like Dr. Newman was saying. Why did he target you?"

"I'm not dead, Asher," Rogan replied. "Hence, not a victim."

"Oh, but you are," Liv said. "Not in the traditional sense, of course. But he's still victimizing you. Controlling you." She snapped her fingers with a realization. "Indoctrinating you."

Rogan looked at her with confusion. "What does that mean?"

"Indoctrination is when someone gets you to conform your worldview to theirs," Asher said.

Amber slapped Asher across the back of the head. "He knows what 'indoctrination' means, jerk." Asher cowed a bit more than necessary.

"I mean that maybe he thinks you're an acolyte, a follower," Liv explained. "Or potentially one. So, he wants to twist you to become his sidekick. And potential replacement."

"Oh, that's good, Liv," Mikey said with excitement. "Like, Killtown was about a competition between killers. But this is about training new killers. Didn't the hack yesterday call it Kill U?"

"I just want to know what this nut job would do if Kingston or King University hadn't had 'King' in the name. That play on changing 'ng' to 'll' is slick marketing," Dex said.

"Well, Kingston and King University were both founded by the King family in the 1800's," Amber explained. "And if he's following my family..."

"Why would your family stay so close, Amber?" Margot asked. "I think you'd want to get as far away from Killtown as possible. Unless... you liked the attention?"

Amber glared at Margot. "How dare you suggest that! My friends died. My parents almost did-"

"Yet they got away," Margot interjected. "And so did you."

"Wait, hold on," Rogan said, trying to calm the tension. "Margot, you're not seriously suggesting Amber is involved?"

Margot shrugged. "Trauma makes you do crazy things."

"Um, guys, we all know it isn't Amber," Mikey said. "She was with us when the cop got killed. And no offense, Amber, but there was no way you lifted that dude up on the building like that."

"Thanks, Mikey," Amber said. Then she took a deep breath. "But I have to say, as offended as I am at Margot's accusation, she's not wrong to start pointing fingers."

"Yes! Time to accuse people!" Asher shouted.

Liv looked at him with judgment, "Why are you excited?"

"Oh c'mon, you all know that part in all the slasher movies where the main cast gets together to accuse each other, but then nothing comes of it until the final reveal?" Asher said.

Blank stares met him.

"Fine," Asher said. The Host has to be someone who has a connection to Killtown. Maybe a relative of one of the killers? Or one of the survivors?"

Rogan shook his head. "All the identified relatives of the killers disowned them. Clute was an only child and his parents are old, like pushing seventy."

"My parents and I are the only Knox family members left," Amber answered. "Mom's sister lives in Kansas and Dad was an only child." She paused, then added, "Well, he is now."

"What about the other guy?" Dex asked. "Claude?"

Amber shrugged. "He's single, his brother was killed in a car accident five years ago, parents are dead."

"What about Claude himself?" Asher asked pointedly.

"He does seem to be enjoying some fame of late," Mikey pointed out.

"And he's a big dude," Liv added.

Rogan countered, "Nah, he's a glory hound and a redneck, but he's no killer. I just interviewed him for the podcast before last- he loves playing the hero too much."

"But what if that's the plan," Margot said. "Killtown had two killers, what if Claude is having his cake and eating it, too? He kills, partner kills, then Claude kills the partner to play the hero?"

"You are dark and twisty for a sorority girl," Mikey said with a grimace.

Margot shrugged, "Psych major."

Their phones buzzed in unison.

Amber looked at her phone and saw the campus-wide alert. Her jaw dropped.

"President Straub was killed!?!" Asher exclaimed.

"We gotta go see this!" Dex said, rising up.

"Wait!" Rogan shouted. "There...there's something else. The Host, he knew about the documentary deal. He knew Amber was in on that. The only people who knew that were in this room, and the documentary people. So that means-"

"That either one of us spilled those beans-" Mikey said.

"Or one of us is trying to up their kill count," Dex said.

The silent tension in the room built as everyone looked closely at each other.

Finally, Amber said, "Or...the Host found out some other way, and will use our distrust to separate us. Either way, I think their visit to Rogan answers one big question we've all been afraid to ask."

"And that is?" Margot asked.

"If we are all targets," Amber said dryly. "And the answer is yes. But we clearly aren't the only game the Host is playing this time."

CHAPTER 10

While crime scene techs continued to process the scene outside, Knox, Claude, Joel, and Cade huddled around the stack of financials that had been stabbed into Holden Straub's chest.

"Yep, fifty-three thousand dollars over the last four years," Knox said. "He was skimming off the books. Good catch, kid."

Cade smiled sheepishly and gave a shy, "Thanks."

"Now, the question is, how did the Host know about this?" Joel asked. "It got past auditors and the financial planner-"

"Ah, no- Straub was handling all of that for some time now," Knox interjected. "One less level of deception. But I missed it, and that's on me."

Detective Joel patted Knox on the back. "Not your job, man. You were supposed to keep an eye out for drunk and disorderlies and abusive boyfriends, not look into the white-collar crimes."

Knox knew he meant well, but the compliment had a barb on it, too. What Knox heard was *You're just a campus cop.*

"So, he was caught with his hand in the honeypot," Claude said. "Who coulda caught him that would be capable of this?" He pointed out the windows to the scene and froze. "We got company, boys," he said ominously.

Four black-suited men walked up to the door and entered the hall outside Knox's office. The lead agent had gray hair and a stern look, and the others were uniform in size if not appearance. One was bald, one was African American, and one sported a thinly trimmed red beard and close-cropped hair to match. Even before they declared it, Knox knew who they were.

"FBI Special Agent Durst, these are my associates from the Houston Field Office, Agents Blakely, Norris, and O'Hara."

"Betcha the ginger is O'Hara," Claude said out loud. The red head glared, but the bald one laughed.

Durst ignored it and continued. "We have been requested to take over the investigation, as it is clearly becoming a serial case. In addition, we were requested by a government official."

Joel squinted at Durst. "The mayor? Chief of Police?"

"By me," came a new voice. A man with brown hair and a thick, brown handlebar mustache walked in. He wore a very expensive suit with an American Flag lapel pin, and removed a tan cowboy hat as he entered.

"Senator King," Detective Joel said.

"Correct," the senator affirmed. "Holden Straub was a friend, and I just spoke with him last night about some school financial matters. When I heard about his death, I called in some favors with the Bureau. Felt they were better equipped to lead the investigation and head off this killer before it gets worse. And, as this university bears my family name, I am very interested in seeing this matter resolved ASAP."

"By 'financial matters,' do you mean Straub's embezzlement?" Knox asked flatly. The senator gave a deadly look to Knox, who simply said, "Sullivan Knox, campus security and former sheriff of Kingston."

"That is a bold and baseless accusation against a good man, Mr. Knox," King said. "You had better have proof to support this claim."

Knox raised a hand and pointed with exaggeration at the papers on the desk. "Fifty-three thousand dollars, and all the data is right here. Of course, you knew nothing of this, Senator?"

The senator flushed and then went from being perturbed to being outright enraged. "I am a United States Senator, not to mention a member of the family that founded this university and your hometown, sir. I will be accorded respect."

"I see why you liked Straub," Knox said. "You were both entitled sons of bi-"

"Alright, let's calm this down, gentlemen," Durst said, stepping between them. "While the

Bureau will take the lead, we want to work with the local law enforcement. We need your knowledge and experience on this case as much as we need your evidence. We would like to be able to set up shop somewhere- and we thought the location of the first murder might provide a space to work?"

Joel looked around the room, then looked at Faust. "That'll work. Detective Faust and I will take you there. It might be good to look over the Killtown evidence as well. See if it adds to this, if this guy is somehow connected to what happened in Kingston." Then he looked at Knox and King, the latter still staring daggers at the former. "Senator, why don't you come with us? Knox and Garvin, you folks secure the campus." He gave them a wink that Knox took to mean 'keep investigating.'

Joel placed the papers back in their evidence envelope, and all of them left the office. As they walked past the scene, King stopped by the body of Ray Oswald. Knox saw a brief moment of recognition cross the senator's face, then he kept moving.

"Sully!" Lindsey called out to him from behind the police line.

Knox made his way over, followed by Claude. He watched as the suited men left the scene, then he turned to his wife. "Feds are taking over," he said.

"Was that Saul King?" she asked.

"Yeah, friends with Straub," Knox answered. "And I don't know if you caught this Claude, but I think he knew the other victim, too."

"Yep, saw that," Claude answered. "King ain't a suspect is he?"

Knox didn't answer. He didn't like the senator, but it wasn't likely he was involved in the murder. Or the embezzlement, based on his reaction to the news. But if he knew the kid and Straub, then the senator might either be a target, or might know information that could put the pieces together. "Not right now, Claude. Say, Lindsey, can you get access to student records? For Ray Oswald? He was the other victim."

"Some, not all. Why?"

"What are the odds he randomly walks up on the killer, and he knows Saul King?" Knox asked out loud. His hand began to shake, and he raised his hand to his head.

"Are you having an attack?" Lindsey asked, concern in her voice. He had been experiencing panic attacks since…Kingston. The stress of the last few days and especially that morning was coming home to roost.

Knox nodded, but then said, "Claude, keep digging. Lindsey, can we talk alone?"

Claude nodded and went off to…do whatever Claude did. "Lindsey, I need to see Doc Crewe."

"Another panic attack?" she asked with concern.

Knox nodded, and Lindsey immediately called to confirm he was in. Since he was, they walked quickly toward Crewe's building on the edge of campus. They were just around the corner when they turned and ran into Amber and her friends leaving the studio. As soon as Amber saw her father, she went pale. "Dad?"

"It's another attack, honey," Lindsey said. "Come help me take him to Dr. Crewe."

Amber looked back at Rogan and the rest, then went to her father and they continued on their way.

"What is it? Is it Straub's murder?" Amber asked. When her mother looked at her, Amber explained, "We all got the campus emergency text."

"That's... part of it... Amber," Knox said through deep breathing techniques to slow his heart rate. "Why were you and your friends meeting?"

"Ah, uh, just...discussing the killings and the threats. You don't think this is escalating to another Killtown thing, do you?" Amber asked.

Until the call that morning about Straub, Knox had held onto the slim hope that the dead cop was a one-off. What happened in Kingston had all been a shell game to hide the real targets- his family. Now, Knox wondered if the shell game was the threat of a repeat of Kingston. What if the killer was really after 'message' victims? Exposing those who were getting away with crimes? Or hypocrisy? Or who were hiding secrets?

Then he recalled a secret he had discovered not too long before that would have put Amber at risk. So, he asked her, "When were you going to tell your mother and I that you and Rogan were doing a documentary?"

Amber's eyes went wide. Lindsey gasped. Then Knox said, "Well, good thing we are going to the therapist. Sounds like we have some stuff to talk about."

❖ ❖ ❖

"How could you not tell us?" Lindsey cried, her voice just shy of a shout.

"I knew you had wanted to protect me when the whole thing went down," Amber said, trying to remain calm. "But I am an adult now, old enough to make my own choices. It's not like I'm agreeing to an interview with a stranger- it's Rogan. You know him. You like him."

"*That* decision is under review," Knox countered. "I had no problem with him when he did his little podcast, distant from this family. But when I found out about the deal-"

Lindsey spun to Knox. "Speaking of which- when did you find out about that and how long did you wait to tell me?"

"Found out yesterday, amid everything else," Knox said calmly. "Got the request from the production company to have access to campus and saw Rogan and Amber listed. Didn't try to hide it- a lot has happened in the last day, Linds."

That calmed Lindsey a bit, and she remembered for the first time that Dr. Crewe was listening in. "Sorry, Dr. Crewe, but I guess you saw the real Knox family."

Crewe chuckled. "Finally. I kid, I kid. But this is good. All of it. Knox, you did the right thing coming here during your attack, and even if it was unintentional, you did the right thing in waiting until now to bring up what you knew. Lindsey, you have every right to feel blindsided by Amber's news, but remember, she is an adult. As she just said. She can make her own decisions- but I think it is important that she talk with you about it. Now, Amber, about the documentary-"

"You don't think I should do it," Amber said dejectedly.

"Quite the opposite," Crewe said with a wave of his hand. "I think you need to."

"What?!?" Lindsey and Knox yelled in unison

"This is her chance to process what happened in a way she hasn't had before," the doctor said. "And with all that is going on, I think that's important for her. Speaking of the murders, I was sorry to hear about Straub. As a faculty member, I...wasn't a fan. But to die that way...so horrible."

"And then there is the evidence of

embezzlement," Knox said out of the blue. Lindsey snapped her head to Knox and saw his eyes intently focused on Crewe. "But then I guess you hadn't heard that yet."

Crewe had a carefully crafted look of surprise fixed on his face. "I had not heard that, no. I must say I am surprised- and yet not. He did like the extravagant lifestyle." Crewe's face became a mask, but Lindsey knew the doctor was more aware than he was letting on. So did Knox. So, he pressed.

"And you know there was another murder," Knox continued. "He looked familiar to me, I thought I had seen him somewhere before, then suddenly, it hit me. I had seen him here. In your office."

Crewe began to shake his head. "You know I can't talk about clients, Sully."

"Ray Oswald," Knox said. Lindsey suddenly realized she *did* know the boy.

"Oh my god," Crewe said. "He was my assistant before Asher..."

"That's right," Lindsey said. "He left about a month after we started seeing you."

Again, Crewe shook his head. "No, he didn't leave. I fired him. He had started taking files, or at least information from files. I suspected he was trying to build evidence for blackmail. But I caught him before he got too much."

"Did he get files on Straub?" Knox said, still glaring at Crewe.

Crewe froze. His breathing slowed. "Yes."

"And Doc, I realize you can't share sensitive data, but might it be important for us to look a little more closely at what Oswald might have taken?" Knox asked.

Crewe nodded.

"Thanks, Doc, I'm feeling lots better. This really helped," Knox said jovially, and then rose to his feet. "I think the other things are best discussed with the family alone. Lindsey, Amber, let's go."

Knox barged out and announced, "See you soon, Asher. And thanks for confirming the documentary stuff when I called yesterday."

Lindsey was walking out behind Amber and saw her daughter give Asher a death glare, and Asher recoiled and mouthed what looked like "What could I do?"

As they exited the building, Lindsey punched Knox in the arm.

"OW! That hurt! What'd you do that for?" Knox yelped.

"Oh, I don't know, faking a panic attack so you could get access to Crewe and get information from him, maybe," Lindsey replied. "And just casually dropping the fact that our daughter had been lying to us!"

"I didn't lie," Amber protested. "I just omitted some aspects of my daily life."

"Besides, I told you as soon as I could," Knox said defensively. "The truth is, I did have a mild attack, but I worked through it. And I needed you all to be in the dark about what I had to ask Crewe. I thought I had seen Oswald before, and if he did take files on Straub, he may have been in on the murder and got cleaned up as a loose end."

Lindsey scrunched up her nose and looked at her husband and daughter. "That was some smart detective work, I guess," she admitted.

"It felt good, you know," Knox said. "Now, I have to decide if I tell the Feds or not."

"Feds?!?" Amber exclaimed.

"Yeah, Straub's buddy is Saul King, the senator. He called in a favor," Knox explained. Then he paused. Lindsey could read her husband well- he suspected the senator of something, but he couldn't put his finger on it. And that worried him. He looked at Amber, "I guess you and your friends have some theories. Who do they think is behind it?"

Amber shifted nervously. "Some of them think it's Claude."

Knox laughed, and Lindsey stifled her own chuckle. "Amber, Claude has come a long way in my estimation, but he just isn't smart enough to pull this off. Besides, he's a good guy. A lifted-truck-driving-hick, but a good guy."

"That's what I said," she agreed, but Lindsey could see something else was bothering her.

"Amber, honey, what else?" Lindsey asked.

"How sure are we that all the killers from Killtown died?"

Lindsey and Knox exchanged a glance, before Sully asked, "Certain, why?"

"Well, they asked about it, the possibility of one surviving, and I dismissed it," Amber replied. "At first. But… I don't know why, but I can't shake the feeling that all this is more than a copycat."

The look on Knox's face made a shudder run down Lindsey's spine. It was a look of agreement with what Amber had suggested.

When he finally spoke, it did little to ease Lindsey's concerns. "They all died, but I do think what happened in Kingston is directly tied to this. And whether we are the intended targets or we just keep getting in front of the actual target, our family needs to be very, very careful."

KILLTOWN, SEASON 2, EPISODE 3

I know I said we were done.

But something happened.

I was...compelled...to continue this podcast.

I promise I will explain, but first, I want to give another first-hand account of events here at King University. You will no doubt have seen that our university president, Holden Straub, was murdered last night. You will also know that a student, Ray Oswald, was also killed. Now, I have from an anonymous source, evidence found by my production assistant Mark when we arrived at the studio today. Evidence of what message was left at the crime scene.

There are many cell phone videos of the crime scene, but you cannot see as clearly as the evidence I hold in my hand now. Straub was stabbed multiple, multiple times. And stabbed into his chest was a stack of papers. From the photo I have, it appears to be financial records. And that's not all- there was a literal message in blood. It says simply, "Follow the Money."

Now, ladies and gentlemen, Killtown, as we know it, was not so much about sending a message as it was exposing secrets. The secrets that the killers, Jane Sharp and Nate Clute, felt were destroying their lives. It appears that the Host- who claims to be back, not a new Host, I should point out- is trying to do the same thing.

Now, this is just conjecture on my part, but the images I received of those financial documents seem to show that President Straub was embezzling money from King University. And the implication is that the Host killed him for his corruption. Sadly, it seems that Ray Oswald was merely in the wrong place at the wrong time. This now brings the Host's count of kills to three here in Nacogdoches.

I fear that this is just the beginning.

You see, as I said at the start, I was compelled to continue the podcast in spite of the murder spree. Compelled is not the right word- I was threatened. Last night, while I slept, the Host invaded my home and stood over my bed. He woke me and demanded that I continue to tell his story. Then he was gone.

In addition to this...nocturnal visit...there was a note attached to the evidence left for me. The note was, as best as I can recall, a direct quote of something the Host said to me last night. It goes like this: *I am not a villain- I am a product of the true villains. Those who create systems that enslave, subjugate, and crush those just trying to survive in it.* End quote.

I know- it sounds too ludicrous to believe. But bear with me. The Host is a showman. We saw that in Kingston. Killtown was a show with its own cast of characters. Each one served a purpose. The killers created chaos and took pieces off the chess board. But the citizens also played a role. One they had no idea about. But the Host made them play, play to the point of death.

Nacogdoches and King University is a fresh, clean board to play. And so there are new pieces. I fear that I am one. I fear what that means for my own longevity. But not only will I continue to tell this story, I will continue the story of Killtown in a new venue. As I record this podcast, cameras are here from a documentary crew, getting footage for a documentary that I hope to release next year. And this, folks, is the last scoop I am giving you today. The star of this documentary is Amber Knox, telling her story for the first time. In her own words.

With the murders starting up again, it is important that we continue to pull the curtain back on the dark doings of the Host. Today, we ask the important question no one has brought up- if this is Killtown 2, where are the other killers? Or is this sequel about winnowing down to what is really important? Let's start with why I think there will be no other killers...

CHAPTER 11

Rogan was turning off the machines when he heard Mark shout, "What are you doing here?"

Rogan looked up and saw four black-suited men with sunglasses marching into the booth. They were followed by Detective Joel, who looked almost embarrassed to be there. One of the two cameramen from the documentary crew was still there, and he whipped his camera up and began filming. Then he slunk back into the shadows, unseen by the new arrivals.

The lead person marched into the booth and demanded, "Are you Rogan Benson?"

"Depends who's asking," Rogan replied.

The man sneered, almost gleeful that Rogan was being snarky. "Good, it's been awhile since I got to teach a punk some lessons. I'm FBI Special Agent Durst, of the Houston Field Office. These are Agents Blakely, Norris, and O'Hara. I think you know of Detective Joel here? Did you or did you not post a podcast claiming to have been visited by the suspect calling themselves 'The Host?'"

Rogan nodded. "I did."

Durst made a face like he expected more.

When it didn't come, he asked, "And why did you not inform the police?"

Rogan chuckled. "Truth be told, I doubted you'd take me seriously. Heck, I didn't believe it myself at first. But he didn't say he was going to do anything else, just that I needed to keep doing the podcast. And...that he'd give me an exclusive."

"There it is," Durst said with satisfaction. "You stood to gain from this whole thing, so you kept your mouth shut. That, young man, is an admission of intent to impede an investigation."

"Now, hold on," Detective Joel interjected. "I think that's going a bit far, Agent Durst. I think Rogan will cooperate-"

"He will, because I am placing him under arrest," Durst said, producing handcuffs. "See, I don't buy his story about his little visit. I think he's involved in the killings because I bet his little podcast is getting a big boost. And didn't you say you had a documentary deal, too?"

"I want a lawyer," Rogan said.

"All the guilty ones do," Durst said as he marched Rogan from the room.

As he passed Mark, Rogan said, "Call an attorney- anyone you can find. And call Amber."

"You got it," Mark said as Rogan was led from the building.

"Hey! There's a cameraman!" shouted the bald agent- Blakely. O'Hara and Norris moved quickly and grabbed him.

"Hey! I have a right to record this!" he

protested.

"Yep, you sure do," Durst said. "But I also now have reasonable doubt that you were helping Benson here cover up evidence. You're under arrest, too." Then he proceeded to read both men their rights.

He was done by the time they burst forth onto the street outside, and bright daylight made Rogan blink. When his eyes focused, they fell on a familiar- if unfriendly- face.

Nikki Meyers.

"I knew it," she spewed with venom. "A depraved mind who digs up the dead will eventually try to create more depravity. I hope you rot in jail. Holden Straub was a good man!"

Her small group of followers began shouting and calling for Rogan's blood as he was placed in the back of a standard black sedan. He sat in the middle of the back seat and turned his head to look at Nikki one last time.

Her expression was one of satisfaction.

Rogan dropped his head into his hands and wondered what he had gotten himself into.

❖ ❖ ❖

As Rogan Benson was being settled into the black SUV, five dark figures gathered around a sixth figure. The sixth wore a hood over his wooden mask, and in the dim light of the space his red eyes somehow managed to glow.

The low, mechanical voice of the Host began to speak. "Welcome, my young recruits, to the new iteration of Killtown. I have called you here because of the potential I have seen in you. You have talents and techniques that need to be refined, and this night will be one of education for you. Before you, you will see your new identities." He waved his hand toward the masks that lay on the table before the five shapes. A domed metal mask sat next to a gas mask. Next to that was a clown mask, a simple ski mask, and finally a blackout hood. "You are now the Brute, the Pyro, the Novice, Mr. Blue, and the Wraith. These masks were once worn by some of the most savage killers the world has seen, and now, you will take on their role. Each of you has a task, a challenge as it were, to complete. Killtown was a competition, but Kill U will be a sort of gauntlet. Survive it, and you graduate with skills to become the bloodthirsty murders I know you can be."

The dark shapes moved forward and took their masks. The silence was broken by the hiss of a re-breather starting up on the Pyro.

"Excellent. Your...final exam...begins an hour after sunset. You have until sunrise to complete your assignments." The Host raised a fist, and one by one the new killers raised theirs. The Host intoned, "We are the Host!"

In unison, all six repeated, "We are the Host!"

❖ ❖ ❖

It surprised Rogan to find that he was not taken to the police station, but rather to the evidence warehouse. The agents driving the car, Norris and O'Hara, explained that their base camp was the warehouse because they wanted to be free of being watched by too many local cops.

"Are all of you FBI guys such dicks?" Rogan asked.

O'Hara chuckled. "Pretty much," he answered.

"Well, I guess acknowledging you have a problem is the first step to healing," Rogan replied.

The car pulled to a stop and Norris came to open Rogan's door. Immediately, he saw three camera trucks racing toward them, trying to get the scoop. "Any chance you boys want to protect my identity here?"

"Nope," Norris said, taking his time getting Rogan from the car. "We're dicks, remember?"

Rogan sighed and watched as Durst and Blakely got the cameraman, Guy, from their car. Joel had pulled up on the other side, as had a fourth vehicle, a black SUV with government plates. A man in a suit stepped out and placed a cowboy hat on his longish brown hair. Then he smoothed out his thick mustache with his fingers and glared at Rogan. A disgruntled Detective Faust got out of the passenger side of the car.

"Ah, Senator King, I see you are a fan of mine," Rogan quipped. It was a mistake.

"You little punk, you killed my friend!" the senator shouted- just as the first of the camera crew had taken aim and started filming.

That sound bite will definitely make the news, Rogan thought to himself as they led him inside. He entered first, followed by Guy, then the senator. And last, the detectives entered.

Rogan was taken into the main room the FBI had set up while Guy was led down the hall to a holding space. The agents shoved him into a chair, and then Durst walked in, turned and ordered Joel and Faust, "Get me the Killtown evidence, I want to look over it."

Joel nodded to Faust, but Durst clarified. "Both of you get it. I want a moment alone with the suspect."

Joel in particular hesitated, but then nodded. He made eye contact with Rogan as if to say it would be alright, then they went down the hall.

So, it was just Rogan and Durst.

And the senator.

Rogan looked at the politician with concern, and Durst picked up on it. "Senator, please do not speak. I am not exactly a fan of you being in here, but, well, you have pull with the right people. So, please do me that favor of silence."

The senator nodded reluctantly.

Durst turned to Rogan. "No cameras, no witnesses, just us. Did you do it?"

Rogan almost laughed. That was the best the FBI could do? But then Rogan remembered he had requested his lawyer. "Lawyer," was all he said.

"Fine, fine. Have it your way. Just know that if you are involved, it would be better to just own up. We can cut a deal that way," Durst offered.

"Oh, okay. Well, since you put it that way," Rogan said thoughtfully. "L-A-W-Y-E-R. Lawyer. En Espanol? El abogado. German-"

"Alright, smart a-"

"Agent Durst, we have a problem!" Faust exclaimed as he burst into the room. "The Killtown evidence, the masks- they're gone."

"Gone?" Durst shouted. "They were here after the cop's murder, weren't they?"

"They were, but when you took over the warehouse, you also sent our officers away," Faust explained.

"That means you left it unmanned, and pretty easily infiltrated," Joel said, barely containing his satisfaction at putting the agent in his place.

"Oops," Rogan said.

Durst turned on him with an animalistic rage, but the phone rang. "Someone get that!" Durst demanded.

Faust grabbed the phone and said, "Nacogdoches Evidence Warehouse, Detective

Faust speaking." Then a look of shock came over his face.

He punched the speakerphone button, and a mechanical, low voice came from the receiver. "Am I on speaker now? Good. This is the Host, and I want to explain to you what is about to happen."

"This is FBI Special Agent-" Durst began.

"SHUT UP! I do not care that you are there Agent Durst. I knew that. That is why I waited to call until you all arrived," The Host said. Durst looked around the room and motioned for Faust to get a trace going. Then he looked at Blakely, who had walked up and motioned for him to do a perimeter sweep. "Now, I believe you are trying to trace me, which makes sense. It's what I would do. But it won't matter. I've made...plans for that." The front door creaked loudly as Blakely, O'Hara, and Norris went to do a perimeter sweep. "And yes, you would be wise to send someone to search the premises, but it will do no good. I am well into my preparation for a most interesting evening." He paused, and there was silence. "You may ask what I mean by that now."

Durst looked around the room, and Faust gave him a thumbs up that the trace was running. "Er, what do you mean by that?"

"Killtown was a competition, but I learned from that experience that serial killers need to be better trained, or they don't last long," the Host said. "Take Sean Densman. Such promise. Alas, then Officer Faust, now Detective Faust, obliterated the poor boy. So, beginning after sundown tonight, I am instituting Kill University, or Kill U for the kids. A whole new crop of killers will test themselves against you. Heh, and against me. But see, they don't know that yet. The indicator of when the competition begins will be a spectacular death, much like Killtown."

"Uh, what do you mean by 'spectacular death?'" Durst asked.

"As you have no doubt noticed, I am playing a game in two parts. I have begun killing those with secrets. I told you of President Straub-"

"How dare you disparage a great man!" King exploded.

"Now, Senator King- can I call you 'Saul?'" the Host responded, nonplussed. "Saul, you would do well to mind your manners with me. I have not yet decided if I want to play with you or let you just be an observer this time. And there are many things about our dear, departed President you didn't know. Or rather, want us to think you didn't know...hmmmm?"

King's face flushed.

"As I was saying, Straub had his secrets. So did Officer Volker and young Ray Oswald. But you will find those things out soon enough. The 'spectacular kill' will be such in a variety of ways. But you will know it when you see it."

"Are you going after the Knox family? And Claude Garvin?" Rogan asked, not caring for a second that he was under arrest and that this call was pretty much exonerating him.

The Host laughed. "Remember how I said I was playing two games?" He paused. "Maybe it is three, after all. Or maybe I just want to spread law enforcement as wide as I can. In any case, I'd be ready, Agent Durst. Consider this the commencement address for Kill U."

The phone went dead, and Faust announced. "No trace. He bounced it off three or four sites per second."

"So, am I free to go?" Rogan asked.

Durst glared at him, then set his jaw. "Not yet. There were two in Kingston, right? Why wouldn't there be two here?"

Rogan sighed.

"Faust, you get out there and start a street search." Durst turned to Joel and said, "Get word to your chief. Blanket the city, every man on the street. Let's end this before it begins."

CHAPTER 12

"I don't care what he says about first amendment blah, blah, blah," Nikki Meyers said harshly into her phone while standing in the checkout line. "King University gets some state funding, our tax dollars should *not* have been supporting smut like that Killtown podcast."

The checker glanced up and made the mistake of making eye contact with Nikki, who was in a foul mood. "Can I help you?" Nikki said with acidity.

The young girl ducked her head and kept sliding the food down the belt. "No ma'am, sorry."

The bagger was placing food into Nikki's reusable bags, and she turned to him just in time to see him put vegetables in the same bag as the boxed goods. "Excuse me, young man, do you know how to bag?" she asked, knowing the answer was of course, 'no.' She muttered in disgust as she turned back to the phone. "Julie, I'll have to call you back. This grocer has hired some of the most incompetent people." Nikki turned back to the bagger and proceeded to explain exactly what goes where.

The bagger had a look that said he'd love to tell her where her advice was supposed to go.

Of course, when the total was rung up, Nikki pointed out that that couldn't be right. "Oh, wait, I have coupons."

A man in line behind her muttered something under his breath. Nikki cut her eyes at him and glared. He too demurred under the Medusa-like gaze of Nikki Meyers.

"Will you need help to your car, ma'am?" the checker asked.

"Well, it's the least you can do for the price of these groceries," Nikki replied. The bagger's shoulders slumped, and he took the handle of the cart and began to follow her out.

Neither of them saw a dark figure standing in the shadows just outside the store entrance. The long shadows of dusk hid the figure well, but Nikki didn't notice because she was back on her call with Julie. "Sorry about that. I guess I shouldn't be surprised. Working for minimum wage makes for minimum mental capacity."

Nikki stopped as a car passed by, then she bolted in front of the next car with her phone stuck to her ear. She ignored the honk of the truck's horn as she continued talking. When she noticed that the cart was not with her, she turned and saw that the boy had stopped to let traffic pass. "Hey," Nikki shouted. "What is your problem, let's go!"

He sheepishly pointed at the traffic and

shrugged.

"Ugh, just give it to me," Nikki snapped, charging in front of the cars again, snatching the cart and darting out once more. "Julie, I just don't think society is much longer for this world. No one is capable of doing anything. And when they do something, they do it wrong or with such filthiness they might as well not have done it."

Nikki continued on her tirade about incompetent workers as she crossed the parking lot. The dark shape followed her at a distance, then ducked behind the car next to hers. A cop car cruised by on the street in front of the grocery store.

"Ugh," Nikki groaned. "This moron parked too close to me." She seemed to ignore the fact that her Mercedes SUV was actually across the line into the other car's space. The driver got out, a Hispanic man, she shouted, "Learn to park, ese!" He looked her up and down, then just kept walking. "Men. I swear, Julie, they can't do anything without us. My husband is just like that. He never does housework, and then has the audacity to say he doesn't because I 'can't be pleased.' Not by him, I say," she cackled into her phone.

She kept talking as she put the last of the groceries in the back of the SUV and closed the door. She turned the cart around and looked for the nearest cart corral. Seeing it was two or three spaces away, she just shoved it in the general direction and went to the passenger side of the car to get in. A dark van with blacked-out windows was parked next to her on that side, and she had more than enough room to get in on that side. She opened the door and began to climb in.

She was halfway across when her foot snagged on something, and she let out a yelp.

"You okay?" came Julie's voice from the phone, which had fallen into the driver's seat.

Nikki looked back and saw that her shoelace had snagged on the knob that moved the seat back. She slid back and pulled it free. Just then the door to the van slid open, and a big man stepped out. She yelped again, and the man jumped back. "Sorry, didn't see you there," he said.

"Yes, well, how you see anything out of that van, I'll never know," she replied.

He too looked her up and down, then walked toward the store.

Nikki climbed back in and found her way into the seat, snatched up the phone and calmed a frantic Julie. They chatted as she backed out of her space, and heard a clang as a cart bounced off her back bumper. "Ugh! These people! Someone left a cart out and it hit my car!" she informed Julie. It did not occur to her that it was actually her cart that had failed to return to the corral.

Eschewing the handheld option, she kept the phone to her ear as she pulled out of the parking lot and onto the street. Behind her, a charcoal gray old truck turned on its lights and began to follow her.

She kept talking to Julie, weaving in and out of traffic, never using a blinker and shouting at other drivers. She did notice an increased police presence, and suspected it had to do with the horrific murders plaguing their once peaceful city. This, of course, returned the conversation to the thing that most irritated Nikki those days, the Killtown Podcast. "I just don't see why the University allows it. Todd and I are donors, by God, and we should have a say." Julie offered that the podcast was publicity, and it did make them some money. "It can't match what the Meyers give. And besides, I started my group, 'Keep Our Airways Pure,' and that is bringing bad press for them. And with the killings, it is so clear that someone is copycatting that horrific tragedy. He was arrested today, so maybe now they will finally cut him off. Especially if he had anything to do with Holden's death." Nikki sniffed the air, fighting the sting of a single tear. It was all she would spare for her deceased lover. He was, after all, still just an average man.

The charcoal gray truck passed her and then signaled to pull in front of her. He had good distance, but when he pulled over, Nikki honked. "Watch it, jerk!" she shouted. "This moron just cut me off, Julie," Nikki said, hitting the accelerator and closing the gap between them significantly. Then she jerked her wheel to the left- again, no signal- and passed him. She gassed the engine and turned to give the driver a patented Nikki Meyers glare, but she froze.

The driver wore a wooden mask.

With red eyes that reflected in the streetlights.

And a saw tooth grin.

Nikki sped past the truck and put as much distance as she could between them. "Stay on the phone with me, Nikki. I just passed a weirdo with one of those wooden Host masks."

Nikki turned off the road at the exit to her neighborhood. She lived outside of Nacogdoches proper, on two acres of land. She loved the distance from town, and the quiet nature of the neighborhood. The truck kept going on the highway, and Nikki breathed a sigh of relief. "I think he's gone, Julie. And I'm almost home, so-"

An explosion of glass and the tearing of metal cut her off. The truck had veered off the highway and come down the embankment, t-boning her Mercedes and driving it off the small country road into a tree. The violence was sudden, and it was over quickly. Nikki felt warm blood running down her forehead, and her arm was inflamed with pain. Her legs were moving, and she didn't feel like anything inside her was broken or damaged. But then terror gripped her. Sandwiched between the truck and the tree, Nikki had no way to get out.

With great hesitation, she turned to look for the driver.

He was gone.

She couldn't see her phone, but she knew it was still on and in the car. She could hear a small voice of Julie calling out. "Julie, call 9-1-1! I'm being attacked!" she screamed frantically. But she had no idea if Julie heard her.

Her radio was still playing, and a crackling sound of static cut into her favorite digital talk radio host. The voice was modulated. The delivery stilted. "Nikki Meyers. You love to judge others. To point out fault, to accuse, to belittle. You sit upon a throne of your own making, wearing a crown of your own design. Yet, you are no king. You are no queen. You are just a sad woman with a lot of insecurity and just enough power to be dangerous. But not dangerous in the right ways. Oh, and you have some secrets, too. I'd ask dear old Holden, but he's...not available for comment."

Nikki's eyes were twitching back and forth, shock was overwhelming her, and her body was starting to shake. And the Host was insinuating he knew about her...relationship...with Holden Straub. "W-who are you?" she asked. She did not see the back door where she had put the groceries begin to rise.

"Oh, you know who I am," the voice answered. "The real question is, where am I?"

Nikki began to look around her, through the spider-webbed windshield and the shattered side windows. There was no one around.

"Where are you?" Nikki cried, tears

streaming down her face.

"Here," came the voice from right behind her head.

She felt a sharp pain in her back as a blade stabbed through the seat and into her kidney. "How does it feel to be judged, Nikki Meyers? To be measured and found wanting?" The knife pulled out, and Nikki did the only thing she could think of doing. She started trying to push the shattered windshield out. All that succeeded in doing was knocking a hole in the window. The knife came down again, tearing into her shoulder.

Nikki whimpered and began to pull herself forward, over the steering wheel, in what appeared to be a vain attempt to get through the windshield.

She realized that her legs were free, and the thought came to her- kick him! She began to kick back at the seat, and she hit something. But it was just the seat. She then began to push her way through the small hole in windshield, first her head, then her shoulders. Each inch forward made the hole bigger, but it came at the cost of a thousand cuts. She was about to her waist when she looked down and saw the amount of blood she was losing, and she grew dizzy. She lost her strength, and fell on the window, impaling herself. She screamed out, pushed herself up, and began to crawl again. Where had the attacker gone?

She finally pulled herself free, and lay on the white hood of her SUV, blood pooling by her shoulder and her stomach. She slid off the hood and down to the ground, then slumped down onto her haunches in front of the car. She looked around, trying to see if the Host was near, but it was quiet.

Dark.

And she was at least a mile from her home.

She began to cry, a screeching, pathetic sound.

But the highway was just up the embankment. Nikki began to crawl for the road. She tried not to look back at the wreck she had emerged from, and when she got to the base of the hill, she had to climb. She could hear the moan of car engines and wheels on the road. She crawled on all fours fifteen feet to the side of the road, and then she stood with much effort, waving for someone to stop.

One car passed.

Two.

The third honked at her, and she heard the man curse at her.

Then the knife went into her spine, and her body went limp. There were flashes of recognition that something was happening to her, but they came and went. She was conscious of being dragged back down the hill, and she saw she was being put upon the hood of her car, her head near the shattered windshield. She couldn't feel her legs or her arms. She couldn't move anything. Her panic rose exponentially when she realized she was paralyzed.

Then that wooden mask was in her face, and the voice said, "You have lived a life of condescension. Hypocrisy. Looking down on all those around you. You felt that you were their better. But here, now, in the end, you bleed just like they do." The blade sliced across Nikki Meyers' throat, and she choked on her own gurgling blood as she looked up to a starry sky.

She died wondering why no one came to her rescue.

She died before she could hear the sirens coming, sirens that resulted from Julie's 9-11 call.

She died never knowing that for all her hate for Killtown, she had been the catalyst to begin the sequel night of Kill U.

It was truly a "spectacular kill."

CHAPTER 13

Reverend Felix Casey was walking through the pews of his small church praying. He prayed for his people to finally see the error of their ways and fully commit to God.

He was praying out loud, so the dark figure that watched him from the darkened hallway heard everything.

"Dear Lord, these reprobate sinners have continued to watch vile, R-rated movies and listen to the Devil's music, even though I have warned and pleaded with them to change their ways. If only they were as holy and righteous as I am, seeking only to please you, Lord." He raised his hands to Heaven and exclaimed, "Oh God, perhaps it would be simpler if you simply sent Your judgment now, and destroyed this wicked, evil world. Those of us who truly seek you will no doubt be spared, by your mercy alone!"

"Are you sure about that, Reverend?"

The voice was a whisper, yet loud enough in the silence for Casey to turn on his heel and locate the sound of the speaker. The dark shape moved into the dim light in the auditorium and the Reverend saw that the figure wore a hood and a blackout mask. "Who are you?" Casey asked.

"The judgment of God," the figure replied.

"Thou shalt not blaspheme in the House of God!" Casey bellowed.

"Funny you should say that," the black-clad figure said. "Seeing as you just claimed to be sinless before God, when I know the things you do in the dark. *Reverend.*" The last word was almost a growl, like the speaker was spitting out something vile.

Casey glared at the person and growled, "You know no such thing, for I do no evil!"

The figure moved forward, seeming to almost glide across the floor. It approached Felix Casey slowly and steadily. "And your internet search history would support that lie? Or expose it? Do your congregants know of your...interest in the youth of the...male variety?"

Casey's face turned bright red. "How dare you-"

"NO!" the voice was still raspy, but suddenly forceful. "How dare *you*? How dare you claim righteousness so boldly when you may just be the most wicked of them all? But the Host is sending us out to cleanse the world of your evil. Your lies. Your secrets."

"Who are you?" Casey asked, the figure now less than six feet from him.

"I am death. I am judgment," the figure said, it's voice a mere whisper once more. "I am the

Wraith."

The figure lurched at the Reverend and suddenly a black blade appeared and plunged into the pastor's chest. Over and over. The attack was quick, but the Wraith savored the kill. The first strike had sent the Reverend into shock, but each stab after that had incapacitated first his arms and then his legs. Escape was impossible for Felix Casey, but so was resistance. "P-please. I never hurt anyone. I- I just looked..."

The Wraith stopped. The knife paused over the Reverend's throat. "I doubt seriously that was all you did," the Wraith said. Then the knife plunged into his groin, and Felix Casey howled in pain. The Wraith drew the knife up from the groin to the midsection and kept slicing all the way up to the chest. Casey screamed the whole time.

Casey lay there on the floor of his church, his chest ripped open and the killer, the Wraith, standing over him, wiping the blood from the blade and flicking it down into his face.

Then he died.

The Wraith grabbed the body by its ankles and drug it to the front of the auditorium, near the lectern that Felix Casey used to rail against the evil in the world. All while he was living in the most evil of fashions. The Wraith turned on the laptop that sat on the lectern, and clicked on an innocuous-looking file, bringing horrific images onto the screen. The Wraith placed it on the body of Felix Casey, then made a phone call.

"There is a body at the Most Holy Church of God, and it is Reverend Felix Casey," the raspy voice said. "He's been a bad, bad man." Then the phone dropped next to the body, the Wraith began to drag the body out of the church.

◆ ◆ ◆

The call about Nikki Meyers was answered by Joshua Joel about two hours after he had left the evidence locker to 'surveil the streets' per the FBI orders. He wanted to call Faust, but he had taken one of the FBI vehicles to collect tapes and recordings from the recording studio then to check in on a couple leads. The FBI still suspected Rogan and was holding him- but they also thought he wasn't acting alone.

So, he called Sully Knox.

Knox knew he needed to be out patrolling, but had made sure there was an officer sitting on his house, where Lindsey and Amber were. Claude had joined him after spending the day trying to find out just what information Ray Oswald had stolen from Dr. Crewe's office.

The three of them were at Nikki's murder scene. Her body was on the hood, and much like with Straub, there was a message in blood. No riddle on that one, though. It simply said, *Hypocrite.*

Claude was explaining what he had learned.

"Wasn't that he took the files, he scanned 'em," Claude said. "Crewe said he could never be fer sure what was taken, or what he just took a pitcher of. But he was sure of one thing…"

Joel looked at him with anticipation. "And that was?"

Claude looked apprehensively from Joel to Knox. Finally, he said, "He took yore family's files, Sully."

"That's it," Knox said storming off to his old black truck. "I'm going to check on my family."

"I'm comin' with ya," Claude announced.

"Wait," Joel said, holding up a hand. "This scene, Nikki Meyers death. Any insight you can give us?"

Knox paused with the door open. "He wrote "hypocrite" in blood on that hood. I bet she had files copied or taken. The Host in Kingston was all about exposing secrets, specifically my family's secrets. This Host is going bigger. Going after people that have an image in the community that they see as a lie. So, anyone with big secrets and a public image is in danger."

Joel's phone rang and he held up a finger. "Joel here…What?" Joel turned to Knox and Claude. "Can your family keep for a minute? Got a call about a body at the Most Holy Church of God. It's about a mile down the road back toward town. They say it's Reverend Casey. Can you secure the scene until I can get uniforms there?"

Knox looked at Claude, who nodded. "Will

do. Let you know what we find."

The two men climbed in the car and Knox pulled onto the access road and began to move toward the turnaround that went under the overpass. "You know this reverend?" Claude asked.

"Only by reputation," Knox said, turning the wheel. "Real old-school preacher. Small congregation, big voice. Why?"

Claude shrugged. "What secrets could he have?"

"Everybody has secrets, Claude," Knox said. "What do you have?"

Claude laughed. "I'm an open book, Sully. Too dumb to keep a secret, you know that."

Knox laughed as well. Claude had come a long way in the last three years. Yeah, he loved the spotlight a little too much, but he was a good guy at heart.

But the laughter stopped when they pulled into the parking lot of the church.

A body was impaled on the wrought-iron fence that ran in front of the property, it was clearly dead, and it was clearly the Reverend. On his chest was a laptop and a phone.

Knox swore.

"Say, doesn't that look familiar?" Claude asked.

Knox put the car in park and got out before he answered. "Yeah. It was how the Wraith was found in Kingston. After Bob Atkins tossed him out the window before he died himself." He approached the body and then felt bile rise in his stomach. "Oh, God," he said as he realized what the images on the computer were.

"Oh man," Claude said. "Guess he did have a secret."

Knox turned away, slamming the computer shut as he did. "Claude, I think I see what's happening here."

"Aside from the fire-n-brimstone preacher being a pedo?"

"Aside from that, yeah," Knox said. "Joel said the masks were gone. The Host has used the phrase 'Kill U' several times. As in Kill University. I think he's training new killers to take on the roles of the original ones. And their final exam is to kill someone that represents the way they were killed in Kingston."

"The Wraith died in a church, at the hands of Pastor Bob," Claude said. "So, this fella had to kill a pastor in a church the same way?"

"Which means that the replacement killers are after archetypes or substitutions of the ones who killed their inspiration," Knox said. "Which means you and I are targets of at least a few of the killers."

"I hit one with a firetruck, Sully," Claude said with a shrug. "So, I just steer clear of firetrucks, right?"

CHAPTER 14

The doorbell rang at Dr. Bennett Newman's house and he jogged down the front hall to answer it. He paused by the mirror in the entryway to brush his hair in place, then opened the door.

Margot Lucas stood there looking tanned and beautiful, pursing her lips and leaning on the doorframe. "Professor, I needed a little extra... tutoring, if that's okay?"

Bennett did a quick scan of the dark street, then ushered her in. As soon as the door was closed, she wrapped her arms around him and they began to passionately kiss. She pushed him up against a wall and ran her hands through his hair. His hands found the small of her waist and gripped her just tightly enough that she felt his strength and pressed her body into his.

After a minute or two of this, Bennett came up for air, and said, "I hoped you'd come by, but with all the murders going on, I worried you'd be too afraid to drop in."

She licked her lips and smiled. "Fear is such a turn-on, don't you think?" He leaned in to kiss her again when he heard a thump come from the back of his house.

"Did you hear that?" he asked.

Margot shrugged and went to kiss him again.

"No, seriously, I heard something," Bennett reiterated, then gently pushed her aside and went to check.

"Benny, you're the one getting freaked out," Margot called after him as she went into the living room and sat on the couch, lounging seductively. "Are you worried the President will find out you are breaking his no fraternization rule? Oh wait, he's dead," she said sarcastically.

Bennett popped his head back in the living room to say, "I could get fired, and you could get expelled, so yeah, I worry about that. Even with Straub gone. But right now, I'm worried about that sound." He ducked back down the hall.

"Afraid the big, bad, serial killer is gonna getcha?" she asked teasingly. "I'm not worried. If little ole Amber Knox can survive the guy, I think you and I will be just fine."

"I appreciate your support, Margot, but this is not something to make light of," Bennett answered from down the hall. "This killer seems more organized than the one in Kingston. I heard on the news there were two killings tonight already. The Meyers lady and they think some local pastor. I just want to be-"

There was a crash from the back of the house, then silence.

Margot sat up, attentive and listening for the first time since she arrived. "Benny? Benny, you okay?" No answer. She stood up and started to walk toward the hallway that Bennett had gone down. At the doorways, she stopped, then peaked around the corner. No sign of him. There was a faint glow coming from the bedroom, and Margot relaxed. "Oh, you're being romantic, I see. A little candlelight, hmm?" She walked down the hall toward the half-cracked door. Outside she could hear sirens in the distance, no doubt going to one of the murders Bennett mentioned. She paused. How had Bennett known about those, anyway? "Hey, Bennett, how did you know about those murders tonight? We haven't gotten a warning from the university or anything."

No answer. "Benny?" she called one last time as she pushed the door open.

Flames rushed to meet her, and she saw that the entire room was engulfed in flame. She didn't see any sign of Bennett, but there was a man in a mask standing amid the flame. A gas mask with mirrored glass eyes turned to look at her, and they raised a hand with a tube attached to the wrist. Flames exploded from it towards her.

Margot fell backward into the hallway and began to crab-crawl her way down the hall. The flames were licking at the door frame and arcing down the hall toward her. She managed to get to her feet and ran into the living room, but she could hear the crackling flame behind her, and a subtle *whooshing* that must have been the flamethrower the arsonist was using. Margot became aware that the sirens were getting closer to where she was and had the clarity of thought to run outside and get away from the killer.

She burst out of the front door and raced toward the street. There was a firetruck coming toward her and she stepped in front of it to flag it down.

The horn blared and she saw the driver slam on the brakes in a frenzy. Then there was a tremendous explosion and the truck lurched onto its side as a ball of flame erupted from the side of the vehicle. Firemen were jumping clear, and the inflamed truck rolled onto its side and skidded past her down the street. She turned back to the house and saw the man in the mask. He was holding a long, smoking tube that she would have recognized as a bazooka if she had ever watched a war movie. The masked man lowered the weapon, then ducked back inside. She stood there in the street, crying and screaming as the firemen who jumped clear tried to rescue their friends from the flaming wreck. Down the street, a dark sedan screeched to a halt and a young man jumped out and ran toward her. She recognized him as that young Detective- Faust, she thought.

"Are you okay?" he asked, taking her by the shoulders.

She was hyperventilating but she turned and saw that he had kind eyes, if a bit dark. "M-my bo- professor...he's inside."

Faust looked around and saw that the firemen were too busy with their own troubles. "I'll go check," Faust said, turning toward the building that was slowly succumbing to flames.

"Wait!" Margot yelled. "There's a guy in a mask- he's the one who started the fire. He's still in there!"

Faust drew his gun and nodded to Margot. He rushed to the door and grabbed the doorknob, shoving the door inward. Flames rushed to meet him, but the Detective ducked away. Then he charged in. Margot watched the door for a minute. Two. Then she heard three clear gunshots. A minute later, Faust rushed out the front door.

Alone.

He was coughing, and his clothes were singed, but seemed no worse for the wear. "No one in there but the guy in the mask, ma'am. I think I winged him, but he got away."

"Where is Bennett?" she asked. "If he wasn't in there, where is he?'

Faust stood up, and a look of understanding crossed his face. "Ma'am, you're a student at the university, friends with Amber Knox?" Margot nodded. He asked, "Did anyone other than your professor know you were coming here?"

"No. Why?" she asked, feeling unnerved. And not because she was afraid her affair with Professor Newman was about to be uncovered.

"I think it best that I get you into protective

custody right away, ma'am," was all he said. He pulled out his phone and hit a few buttons. As he did, he put his hand on her shoulder. It was still hot from grabbing the door. Then she could smell burning flesh. "Joel? Yeah, it's Faust," he was saying. "I've got one friend of Amber Knox. I think we were right; they are a target. I'll try to round them up and get them to a safe-house...Knox is at the church scene? Okay...I'll let him know the plan. This house fire at 513 Wagglin is most likely part of it all."

As he hung up, Margot asked him, "Did you burn your hand on the door?"

Absently, Faust looked at his hand and instantly shook it off. "Ow, yeah, oooh. I guess the adrenaline is wearing off. Ssss. Yeah, that hurts. Let's get you in the car and away from here, and me some antibiotic cream. I have a first aid kit in the car."

He ushered her toward the car as a second fire truck arrived.

The house was totally consumed in flames by that point.

And there was no sign of Bennett Newman.

❖ ❖ ❖

Rogan sat in the interrogation room and waited. The FBI guys had been in and out sporadically, and when the door swung open, he had been treated to snippets of chaos.

"-car run off the road and then slaughtered-"

"-slashed to death. In a CHURCH!"

"-and burns down a house? Any sign of Bennett?"

"-multiple suspects, all over town-"

When Agent Durst returned with the senator in tow, the look on his face was one of embarrassment. "Okay, kid, it looks like you might be in the clear after all," he said as he fumbled with the handcuff keys and walked over to where Rogan sat. "It's madness out there. Fires, car accidents-"

"Dead pastors?" Rogan asked.

Senator King cast a suspicious glance at him, and Rogan smirked. "Relax Sherlock, I hear things when you open the door."

"Actually, Rogan, we...um...well, we wanted to ask you some questions about Killtown," Durst said sheepishly.

"This is a bad idea, Agent," the senator cautioned.

Durst waved him off. "Sheriff- or rather, former Sheriff Knox seems to think the killers are recreating deaths from Killtown. Just in reverse."

Rogan looked at them thoughtfully. "How so?"

"Well, the pastor- Felix Casey- he died in his church," Durst explained. "But his body was found impaled on a fence."

"That's how the Wraith died in Killtown,"

Rogan confirmed.

"That was all it took for Knox to see a connection," Durst said. "Hate to admit it, but he's a smart guy, apparently. Anyway, at the fire, the assailant was seen wearing a gas mask and he fired," Durst laughed darkly, "A rocket launcher at a fire truck."

Rogan's eyes went wide. "Well, the Pyro was killed by Claude Garvin, driving a firetruck, so it's a leap, but I see the connection."

"So, what we need to know is how the other killers died,
Durst asked. King huffed in the back of the room.

"Well, um. Okay. So, those were the first to die, then came the Brute. But that wasn't until the end, in the mill. Knox killed him with the mill saw and a headshot. Then there was Mr. Blue. The Clown. He was killed by the Novice- Sean Densman- on accident. Sean fell on him from above. Saved Sean, killed the clown. Then...the first Host- Nate Clute. Shot by the other Host- Jane Sharp. Then Jane died when Amber Knox hit her with a sledgehammer and Sully Knox shot her. She fell as well. Then Sean, who had escaped, was killed by then Officer Faust with a shotgun."

"How...how would that translate? I mean, tonight. How would the killers change it up and still honor the first killing?" Durst asked.

"This is ridiculous," King said, and he stormed out the door and then out of the building.

"Well, Knox and Amber are still alive- but

the Pyro didn't go after the man who killed his predecessor. Just the method of death- or the tool."

"So, the Brute wouldn't go after Knox necessarily, but something similar?" Durst questioned, genuinely processing.

"Yeah, like maybe he would go to a sawmill, but who would be there at night?" Rogan queried, thinking out loud. "So, I'd still look at any sawmills in town. But maybe it's more about the weapon or the job of the person." Rogan paused. "I mean, he could target a cop? Where is Detective Faust and his partner?"

"Joel is at the Meyers' scene, but heading back soon," Durst said. "Faust was at the fire, but he was then going to round up Amber Knox's friends because one of them was at the fire-"

"Wait- who was at the fire?" Rogan interrupted.

"Uh, a girl," Durst said, looking at his phone. "Named Margot Lucas-"

"Whose *house* was it?"

"A professors'- Bennett Newman." Durst said. "Why?"

Rogan ran a hand through his hair and sighed. "Newman is our criminology professor. A cool guy all around. Amber, me, Margot, Dex, Asher, Liv, and Mikey. But...okay, look, this is just...conjecture. Some of us suspected Margot and the Professor were...involved."

Durst smiled, and it made Rogan uncomfortable. "As in she was there for more than just extra credit?"

Rogan made a disgusted face. "Uh, yeah. Wait- did I hear that Newman was missing?"

Durst nodded. "Yeah, the girl said he went to check a noise, never came back, then the house went up."

"Huh," Rogan said.

"Suspect?" Durst asked, raising an eyebrow.

"Dude, at this point, other than you and me in this room, and probably the Knox family, everyone is a suspect. And if the new Brute is going after cops- you better warn them all. Especially Faust and Joel."

◆ ◆ ◆

Saul King climbed into his SUV and sat for a moment. Then he let out a yell of rage and pounded the steering wheel. That obnoxious kid podcaster was off the hook, and Saul hated it. The punk was guilty of stirring all this mess up, in his book. He sat for a moment, thinking. Where should he go? Out of Nacogdoches, probably. It wasn't safe there anymore. He could head back to his house in the country or-

His seat lurched forward, and he felt a sudden pain in his back. "What the-?" he asked, then looked down and saw the tip of a blade appear through his shirt, near his left shoulder. He began to gasp, and he looked into the rearview mirror to see a metal mask, and behind it, two dark eyes stared back- soulless and dead. Then the blade jerked back and out of his body. He could not move as the man in the backseat climbed out, and went to the driver side door. He opened it and unceremoniously pulled King from the car, dropping him on the ground. The man in the metal mask checked to see that the keys were in the ignition, then he started to climb in and start the car.

Saul King lost consciousness as the car was backing up.

◆ ◆ ◆

Rogan and Durst were in the middle of discussing how the murderers might strike next, when the building shook with a tremendous crash. The lights flickered and the sound of rending metal screeched in their ears. The wall by the entrance, where minutes early Senator King had stormed out, buckled as a massive force rammed into it.

"Get down!" Durst yelled, pulling his weapon from its holster. He ran to the door and tried to open it, finding it to be jammed with whatever had run into the building. He looked at Rogan and then around the room, his eyes landing on the window. "Stay here, you'll be safe. I need to see what's going on." Durst opened the window and climbed up, sticking his head out. He looked back and forth, then looked back in. "Someone rammed Senator King's car into the building. "I'm going to check-"

Durst flew through the window as a hand grabbed his shirt. His body didn't fit perfectly, and Rogan saw his sleeves tear and blood gush as he was yanked forcefully from the building. Rogan heard the sound of metal on stone, and then a wet *thunk*, followed by low moans.

Then a metal mask appeared in the window. Dead eyes looked at Rogan, then vanished.

Rogan scrambled as far from the window as he could get, and looked for anything he might defend himself with.

◆ ◆ ◆

Agent O'Hara was the first to get to the entryway, and all he could see was the wrecked wall and totaled SUV. "You guys stay back, cover me," he said. Then he called out, "Durst, you in there?"

Getting no response, he proceeded to go around the car. He could tell the entrance to the room was blocked. "Durst?"

"Durst is dead," came Rogan's voice. "I think. He got pulled outside by a guy wearing the Brute's mask."

"Stay there, I'll-"

O'Hara barely saw the metal mask rush at

him, and never saw the ax swing up and catch him under the chin. His head flew back as blood, teeth, and bone sprayed up. As his body fell back, the machete stabbed through his stomach and hooked upward into his chest. His head lolled down and looked into the mask as his killer rushed his fellow agents.

They began to open fire, but in their shock, they put more rounds into O'Hara than anything else. The Brute shoved O'Hara's body into Norris, then swung the machete toward Blakely. It cut an arc across his upper chest, and the agent stumbled. Norris tried to bring his gun hand up, but the Brute swung the ax and embedded it in Norris's chest, then grabbed the gun with his now free hand. With surprising strength, he pulled the arm down, and then with the machete severed the hand. Blakely screamed in terror and pain as Norris' blood sprayed him in the face. Overcome, he turned and ran into the darkness of the records room, blood pouring from his chest.

A bullet pinged off of the Brute's mask, and he turned to face Norris, who held the gun up with a shaking grip in his one remaining hand. The Brute walked over nonchalantly and jerked the ax free. He drew back and swung it at Norris- but missed the neck. He did take off the top of the agent's head, though.

Turning to pursue Blakely, the Brute moved into the darkness, listening intently. But mainly, he followed the blood trail.

He found Blakely curled up next to the wall, pleading. "P-please. Don't-"

The Brute brought the machete down again and again, blood splattering all over the wall and his mask. He turned slowly and walked back to the front of the building, the lights still flickering and sparkling on his bloodied mask.

A bullet scraped his left arm, then a second hit him full in the chest. He kept going. He had protection from that sort of thing.

Durst stood firing at the Brute, a deep gash in his chest, and blood covering his body. His face was pale and gray from blood loss, and his vision was unfocused. So, his shots went wild.

The Brute walked right up to him and swung the machete once more. This time, it sailed right through the soft flesh of Durst's neck, and the agent's head bounced off the side of the ruined SUV and fell to the ground. His body followed.

The Brute tore the blood covered cloth from his upper body and dropped it on the ground as he marched into the night. A dark shape stood at the edge of the lights of the evidence building, the Brute nodded and walked on.

The dark shape nodded back.

◆ ◆ ◆

The sound of screams, gunshots, and death had been over for a few minutes when Rogan decided he had to do something. He had been staring at the window for a few minutes, and finally worked up enough nerve to try to succeed where Durst had failed. He cautiously approached it, and called out, perhaps ignorantly, "A-any killers out there?"

Hearing no response, he decided to give it a go. He reached his hands up to the window frame, but as soon as they touched it, he jerked them back like the window was a burning flame. Images of knives coming down on his hands played through his mind. "You couldn't do a podcast about sports or politics, could you Rogan?" he asked himself. Then he steeled his nerves and gripped the window. He took a deep breath, then raised his face to the window. A moderately cool breeze struck him, and he dared to open his eyes.

Nothing.

He looked to his left and saw the tail end of the SUV sticking out of the building. Then, to his right he saw darkness around the side of the building. He looked down and saw that the drop was not too bad. He also saw a pool of blood, but he chose to ignore that.

Rogan pushed himself up and through the window, pausing as he was halfway out. "No turning back now, Benson." He twisted his body so he could get his legs out and be positioned to land on his feet, rather than his head. Then he dropped to the ground, landing in a crouch.

"Nice shot, Rogan!" came a voice from the dark

"What the f-"

"It's me, Rogan," came what was clearly Guy's voice. He stepped from the shadows, a small light blinking from the camera strapped around his head. It was one of those versatile cameras that also had wi-fi connectivity. Rogan saw the blinking green light that meant it was streaming at that moment. "I got out my window after the big guy left and decided to shoot some footage."

"Man, how can you think about the documentary at a time like this?" Rogan asked, catching his breath.

"I'm from Hollywood and I'm dead inside," Guy responded. "Hey, I saw something when the guy came out-"

BANG!

Guy dropped to the ground and a trickle of blood came from a small hole in his forehead, just below the camera.

Rogan turned to see where the shot had come from and stared in horror as a dark figure emerged from the shadows, holding a gun.

The figure was dressed in black, with a tattered cape and a black hoodie. The sawtooth grin and red eyes of the Host stared at Rogan as he said, "Now he's dead outside, too." The Host shoved the pistol into his waistband, then added, "Now, with him out of the way, we can get down to business, Rogan." He bent over Guy's body and began to remove the camera from his head.

Rogan wanted to run, but his knees felt like

jelly. He sank to his knees and begged, "Please, don't kill me."

The Host laughed in his hollow, mechanical manner. "Kill you? No, Rogan, you're going to make me famous. And maybe yourself, too. Now, let's get started." He walked toward Rogan, holding the streaming camera in his hands.

"Started?" Rogan asked.

"Why yes. Started with principal photography on the documentary, of course."

KILLTOWN, SEASON 2, EPISODE 4

Indecipherable clicking, grunting and shifting. Camera comes into focus. It is a dark room, there is nothing that might identify the room. The camera focuses on a figure wearing a wooden mask, with red, shiny eyes. A saw blade grin with dark, burned wood around the mouth speaks, without moving.

Wooden Mask: Ah, there we go. Hold the camera steady, Rogan. Ladies and gentlemen, I am the Host, and my reluctant but capable camera man is Rogan Benson. He has guided you through my story so far, using his podcast, but I believe that my story is best told in the visual medium.

Rogan: (*off camera*) Untie me!

The Host: Now, Rogan, keep your voice down so you don't interfere with my audio. Or I will duct tape your mouth shut. And keep your head still so the camera can focus. Now, about me. You see,

Rogan has truly done an excellent job sharing my story. So good that I had to co-opt his podcast and send it out to my...heh...followers. It took some intricate web skills to create a clone of his podcast and share it to *my* medium in addition to all you regular...what do you call your listeners, Rogan? I'll call them Killheads. That works. Anyway. The medium where my story began, where I conceived Killtown as a concept. See, like the Killtown podcast has said, I discovered my clan, my tribe, if you will, on the dark web. In the darkest corner for serial killers and depraved minds. The Host- or should I say, Hosts- pulled us together. Gave us a place to gather. Then, one day, they offered us a competition. Killtown.

Rogan: So, you are not claiming to be the first Host?

The Host: (*laughing*) Of course not! No, Nate Clupe and Jane Sharp are dead. Really dead. But the Host is more than just them. In fact, the Host is more than just me. *We are the Host.*

Rogan: (*fearful*) You and I?

The Host: (*Laughing*) Perhaps in some manner of speaking. You have helped to make me what I am. Moderately famous. But no, Rogan Benson, I refer to those very much like me. Killers and dark souls who long to shed the blood of others. Those who have followed along with your podcast on my little corner of the dark web, listened to *my* commentary about the story, and learned. And my, how the audience has grown. Now, I publish this interview, and the events that will soon unfold, live on the dark web. But also, on a special channel that *all* can see.

Rogan: Th-the other killers in Nacogdoches- are they the Host? Are they part of this?

The Host: (*Long pause*) You can say that. They are learning, too. But the lesson they are learning is different. It has more to do with vengeance. The Host is about exposing corruption and lies. Then making those who engage in those acts pay. That really is my message, Rogan. That the powerful people who build empires of success on the shoulders of our failures *because* of *their* deceptions can and should be made to pay. I think that message resonates with a lot of people these days, don't you?

Rogan: You said you were teaching them? Are you...training killers?

The Host: Yes. That is why tonight is not really Killtown part two. It is Kill U- a whole new thing. And it is almost time for our next lesson. This time, one of our Kill U students will livestream their attack. So, I will be needing this- (he rises and approaches the camera)

Rogan: Wait- who are they going after?

Off camera there is a dull thunk, and then a shaking

of the camera. Then the camera shifts and the screen fills with the mask of the Host.

The Host: No, Rogan, that would be cheating. See you soon, everyone. We are the Host!

The screen goes blank.

But thousands of computers around the nation ping and thousands of people went to see what the message was. They tuned in to the interview in dank basements, dark sheds, filthy rooms.

Not to mention a few well-appointed studies and cozy living rooms.

Every one of them began to watch and wait for the Host's instructions, his lesson.

It was not just these dark souls that watched the interview, oh no. It spread across social media. It popped into the inbox of Rogan Benson's podcast followers. It was delivered to anti-government groups, and message boards that disgruntled employees come to in order to share their hate.

It reached teenagers who followed social justice influencers advocating violent protests against the powers that be.

And many, many people sat waiting for the next installment. Waiting for the lesson in murder that was promised to come.

Kill U's class was about to be in session.

CHAPTER 15

Knox was speeding back from the church toward his home when he passed the evidence warehouse and slammed on his brakes.

He saw the black SUV in the front of the building and knew it had to do with the killings around town. He pulled a U-turn and drove back.

Claude had hitched a ride to get his own vehicle when they left the church, so Sully sent him a text to go check on Lindsey and Amber, he'd be there soon. Then he pulled his gun and walked toward the building.

He saw blood on the ground and a body. He went to check it, and confirmed the person was dead. Knox didn't recognize him, but he had a black jacket with the name "Guy" and the words "Audio/Visual" embroidered under it. Slowly, Knox approached the SUV. He saw a second body in the passenger seat, but cleared the vehicle before going around to the passenger side to check it. He opened the door slowly, keeping the gun trained on the body.

Immediately, he recognized Senator Saul King. Knox swore under his breath, but then the senator stirred. Knox shook the man's shoulder and saw the deep bruise across his temple. Alarm bells went off that if they didn't kill him, there was a reason. That was when he knew he needed to call Detective Joel.

"Joel, they hit the FBI," Knox said flatly when the detective answered. "Senator King is injured, but alive."

"Holy-" Joel replied. "The agents? Benson?"

Knox slowly approached the ruined entrance and immediately saw a headless body. Then he located Durst's head. Blood spray was all over the walls that led to the door to the warehouse, as well as two more bodies that had been brutally murdered. Both agents.

"One dead civilian, a cameraman- no sign of Rogan, but still clearing the building," Knox replied. "But we are gonna need some more FBI guys."

Joel swore. "I'm on my way. Can you hold the scene? Again?"

Knox sighed heavily. "I need to get to my family, Joshua. Claude is on his way, so I can hold for a bit. Please hurry."

"Understood," Joel said. "Faust is rounding up Amber's friends, I can have him grab them, too, if you want."

"Let's see who gets there first," Knox replied.

◆ ◆ ◆

Amber was in the kitchen with her mother, both trying not to think about the chaos that was surely going down around them.

Her father had texted that Claude was on his way because he got caught up with another incident, but Amber knew what 'incident' meant.

Murder.

She was also trying not to worry about not hearing from any of her friends. Texts were not being returned, and while that was not abnormal with her generation, the circumstances of that night worried her.

It had not escaped her mind that they might be targets. And, sadly, like an uncomfortable itch she could not satiate, it had not escaped her mind that one or more of them might be involved. Wasn't that how it always was in those situations? Wasn't it always someone you knew?

"He'll be here soon, honey," Lindsey said calmly. "And we are safe here. The house has alarms, and heaven knows your dad has fully trained us in what to do in case of intruder."

Amber laughed. Since Killtown, they had taken to having drills. It irritated both Amber and Lindsey, but they knew the intent was good. Amber also knew it stemmed from her father's feelings of inadequacy. She knew he had struggled since Killtown, and when her mom had written the book, he had not been happy. Therapy had been as much about their marriage as it was about their PTSD. Once they got through their mutual trust issues, her parents had been okay. But her dad was a man who felt he had little left to offer the family.

Amber knew that wasn't true. So did Lindsey.

"He is getting better, right?" Amber ventured.

Lindsey looked at her daughter, setting down the knife she was using to cut bell peppers. "He is," she said slowly, genuinely thinking. "He's just not used to being an observer of life. He's a doer. Sully always has been."

Amber bit her lip, and then asked cautiously, "Has he been...different...since the killing started?"

Lindsey sized her up, then asked, "Why?"

Amber shifted uncomfortably. "Do- do you think he...does he seem like he has purpose again?"

Lindsey sighed. "He does, doesn't he? I am terrified that he is out there, but it's almost like this has...healed him."

Amber was about to ask if that scared her mother, but the doorbell rang. "Probably Claude," Amber said, then went to the door. But when she opened it, it wasn't Claude. It was Dr. Crewe. He smiled, and with one hand brushed a stray hair from his face. "Dr. Crewe, we weren't expecting you!" she called out loudly.

Lindsey popped her head out from the

kitchen, "Dr. Crewe, to what do we owe the visit?"

"Well, I wanted to check in," he said, somewhat sheepishly. "Considering what I have been hearing on the news tonight, I suspect you must be a bit anxious."

"Dad's out there, helping the cops," Amber explained, ushering him inside and pointing to the living room. "I'm more worried about that."

He looked at Lindsey and asked, "So, you aren't worried about being targets?"

"I mean, yes, we are," Lindsey said, wiping her hands on her jeans. "But even if these murderers are modeling themselves on Killtown, so far they haven't come after us."

"Except for Amber at school, right?" Crewe said, looking at Amber as he sat on the couch.

In the madness of the last few days, Amber had almost forgotten. "Why would he do that? Make that threat, then just…not come after me?" Amber asked. Lindsey suddenly seemed very concerned, and Amber wondered if she had forgotten about the texts, too.

Crewe shrugged. "I can't say for sure, but maybe he just enjoys toying with you. Maybe it was misdirection, to get the investigation pointed elsewhere. Maybe…" Crewe trailed off.

Lindsey spoke forcefully, and Amber noticed she was looking at Crewe with something that resembled suspicion. "Maybe what?"

"Maybe you are the endgame, Amber," he said with reluctance. "Maybe you're the…what's that trope? Ah, final girl." Something in the way he said it hit Amber wrong. And she felt what her mother must have felt.

"Why are you here, doctor?" Amber asked.

Crewe blinked, and rose quickly. "Wait- sorry. I...I realize that came off wrong. Look- I'll leave you to dinner. Please- call if you need anything."

He turned and walked toward the door, then stopped and turned. "I am sorry- these murders...well, I suppose it doesn't matter now. They have all been my patients, you know. And I... I'm just a little out of sorts. Forgive my intrusion."

Crewe opened the door and standing there was a man wearing a mask.

A clown mask.

"Ding, dong," the clown said in a sing-song voice- the voice so much like Mr. Blue, the clown of Killtown. Then he said, "Ditch!" and shoved Crewe, running away into the night.

Crewe stumbled backward, then turned and looked at Amber and Lindsey- terror on his face and blood in his hands, gripping his stomach.

He fell to his knees and Lindsey rushed toward him. Amber ran to the door, slamming it shut and deadbolting it immediately.

"Amber- call 9-11 and get the gun your father keeps in the living room," Lindsey said, grabbing a pillow and putting pressure on Crewe's stomach wound.

Outside, there was a loud shout, followed by

a few blasts of gunfire. Amber fumbled her cell phone out of her pocket and was about to dial the number when a loud banging at the front door startled her, and she dropped the phone.

"Lindsey, Amber, it's Claude!" said the voice at the door.

"How do we know?" Amber called out. "What if you have one of those voice changer thingies?"

Lindsey whispered, "Get the phone and call, Amber, hurry!"

As Amber picked up the phone and pressed send, the voice replied, "In the Kingston Gazette, they took out ads fer people's birthday. When I turned forty, mine was 'Claudy, Claudy, look who's forty!" and my baby picture had me in…a Care Bears shirt."

Lindsey stifled a laugh in spite of the situation. "It's him. No one would know that that wasn't from Kingston."

As Amber went to the door, the operator answered, "9-11, what's your emergency?"

"Someone with a clown mask and a knife just attacked my psychiatrist at my house." She unlatched the door and started to open it.

"You really shouldn't trust the voice at the door," the operator answered, their voice turning into the voice of Mr. Blue. "Anybody can get those voice changers."

But it was too late, and the door swung open-

And revealed Claude.

Amber screamed, and he rushed in, slamming the door behind him. "I think I winged 'em, but he's got a gun, too," Claude explained. "That the police?" he asked, indicating the phone.

Amber couldn't answer, but she shook her head. Claude took the phone and said, "Git him and yerselves to a closet or somethin' and do it fast. He's gonna try to get in."

Lindsey looked at Crewe and asked, "Can you move?"

He nodded, "I think so, it's not too- ow, ow, ow- deep."

Claude was on the phone as Amber helped her mother lift Crewe up. "Who is this?" Claude asked.

Amber and her mother rushed up the stairs as the sound of crashing glass from the back of the house caused them both to scream.

◆ ◆ ◆

Knox was speeding through the streets, trying repeatedly to reach Lindsey or Amber. But their phones went straight to voicemail. In the distance, he could see the smoke rising from the house fire. The radio crackled with the reports from the Meyers accident and the church murder.

It was as if all Hell had broken loose.

"Not again," Knox grunted as he gripped the wheel and pressed the accelerator down.

❖ ❖ ❖

"You ain't him- or them. We kilt them." Claude said defiantly.

Standing before him the kitchen was a man in black robes, and a hoodie covering a clown mask. THE clown mask from Killtown. Claude could see the dark brown blood stains set against the faux blue grease paint.

The clown's face tilted, ever so slightly as the lilting voice spoke. "Did you now? Or did you simply kill the bodies? The corporeal forms that housed the idea that we were." The clown took a step closer, a gun in one hand, a black knife in the other.

"I'd say gettin' crushed by a fallin' body will do you in nice," Claude replied, training his gun on the clown. "But just in case-" he fired twice and the clown jerked backward and fell to the floor.

"Aw, that was too easy," Claude said, slowly inching toward the body. As he approached, he immediately saw that the clown wore body armor. He raised the gun toward the head, but before he could shoot, the clown kicked out and knocked the gun from his hand. Then he rolled to his feet and jammed the knife into Claude's gut, shoving him backward and pulling the knife from his body.

"Really, Claude?" the clown said mockingly. "You just said it. 'Too easy.' But you know what?

People- they are easy to kill- as you will soon discover. But ideas? Oh, those are rather infinite. You might say that there is a whole...Host...of ways for the idea of me to live on."

"So, you are just a copycat," Claude said, backing away and looking for a weapon. "Just someone lookin' for a bit of fame."

"Now, now, let's not get hypocritical, Claude Garvin," the clown sniped. "Haven't you enjoyed the limelight a bit of late?"

"Screw you," Claude barked. His hand found a loose newel post by the stairs, and he ripped it free. Then he lunged at the clown and must have caught him by surprise. The wooden dowel thudded dully across his face, and the clown staggered back.

Claude drew back for another swing but the clown reached to his side and produced a second knife, and flung it toward him. It embedded in his chest, deep enough to take the wind from him. Claude dropped the post and stumbled back, crashing on the stairs.

The Host stalked forward, sheathing the black knife. He stopped and turned back to where he had fallen. He picked up his own gun. "I don't think copycat is the right word, either," he said, sliding the gun into a makeshift holster on his belt. "I prefer the term...evolution." Then the gloved hand rose to the clown mask and pulled it away to reveal a black ski mask, showing only his dead eyes. The other hand reached behind his back and slipped another mask on- a wooden mask. The mask of the Host. "And I am now so much more. Soon, everyone will learn that."

Claude smiled, blood covering his teeth and dripping from the side of his mouth. "Yer jest a murderer. Playin' dress-up cuz you ain't creative enough to do your own thing."

The Host's head tilted to the side and said, "Your taunts mean nothing. You're already dead."

Claude laughed again, then with his last bit of defiant strength said, "Welp, you'll be joining me soon enough."

The Host pulled the knife from Claude's chest and stabbed him several more times. As he panted from exertion, he watched as the life left Claude Garvin's eyes, and they slowly glazed over, then unfocused.

The Host stood, wiped the blood from the knife, then mounted the stairs. He paused, slipping the mask of the Host off, and replacing Mr. Blue. In the clown's voice, he sang out, "Oh Mrs. Knox, Amber? Come out, come out wherever you are."

◆ ◆ ◆

Faust had deposited his witnesses at the designated location, and now he was arriving at the Knox house. He pulled into the driveway, as close as he could to the house, and turned the car off. Instantly, he could tell something was wrong. He exited the car, drew his gun, and began to walk around the house. Faust thought he saw movement inside the house, and as he approached the back door, he noticed damage had been done to it. The glass was broken, and the door was open. He walked in. Immediately, he saw the body of Claude Garvin on the stairs. He checked for a pulse, but there was nothing. Slowly, Faust mounted the stairs.

It was silent upstairs, not a peep. Not a creak. Also, not a glimmer of light. And he had left the flashlight in the car- rookie mistake.

Even in the dark, he could see a dark stained trail of blood going up the carpeted stairs. If Faust could follow it, so could the killer.

He cleared his corners and kept following the blood trail.

He never saw the dark shape come up from behind him. It grabbed him and threw him into the wall, shattering family pictures and lacerating his face with glass. It punched him in the stomach, then pushed him to the floor. He rolled and saw just in time that a black boot was coming down on his face.

But it still wasn't fast enough to avoid the impact, and Faust was out.

◆ ◆ ◆

Amber, Lindsey, and Dr. Crewe were huddled in the master closet, but they could clearly hear the sounds of the struggle outside.

"Did you ever get the gun?" Lindsey asked.

Amber shook her head.

Crewe was fading in and out of consciousness. And was still bleeding. A lot. Amber followed the trail from his stomach to the door of the closet. And then she realized.

"Blood trail," she whispered.

Lindsey saw it then, too.

The door to the closet flew open, and standing before them was Mr. Blue. He cocked his head to the side and said, "Ladies, it is time to play a game. Dr. Crewe gets a reprieve, thanks to a new arrival. Now," Mr. Blue pointed a gun at them. "Let's stand up and get moving. And I would appreciate it if you put these blindfolds on. Can't have you knowing where I'm taking you and so spoiling the surprise. And, as a bonus, I may have made a bit of a mess downstairs. Wouldn't want you to fret about the state of your carpet, Mrs. Knox."

They covered their eyes with the black cloth, and then walked down the hall, avoiding someone on the floor according to Mr. Blue's directions, then down the stairs. He cautioned them to step around 'a friend' and then he led them outside.

They heard the sound of a car door sliding open, a van door, and they were pushed inside. Mr. Blue deftly cuffed their hands to something metal inside the car, then said, "I'll be right back." A few minutes later, the front door opened and there was the sound of grunts and groans as Mr. Blue put something in the car with them.

The engine revved, and they felt the car begin to move.

Amber began to cry, but she also began to think of how she could possibly get out of the van alive, with her mother.

KILLTOWN SEASON 2, EPISODE 5

The camera came on and showed a nice, two story home. Lights were on inside, and the camera approached the home rapidly. Audio began to pick up voices just as the camera reached the door.

The door opened and there was a man with a look of shock on his face. The person with the camera said in the voice of Mr. Blue, "Ding. Dong… Ditch!" and then the camera fell to the stabbing.

The camera turned and ran to the dark side of the house, but someone shouted at them. Someone who was speaking with a heavy Southern twang.

The camera turned to see Claude Garvin, well known to fans of Killtown, with his gun drawn and shouting. There was a gunshot, the camera shifted sharply, and then from the cameraman, there was another gunshot fired back at Garvin.

The big man ducked, and the cameraman got away.

It was dark, and the camera was low to the ground, stalking around the side of the house. The cameraman was low to the ground, seeking cover by the bushes that clung close to the house. The view went up and saw a glass back door.

The camera slowly rose and approached the door. Viewers by this time were tuning in by the thousands, and they saw the scene inside the house pretty clearly. The big guy, the wounded guy, the middle-aged mom, and the young woman. Frantic.

The window shattered, and a black gloved hand opened the door. The camera stepped into the room. Then Garvin approached with his gun drawn and was speaking.

Garvin: You ain't him- or them. We kilt them.

Mr. Blue: Did you now? Or did you simply kill the bodies? The corporeal forms that housed the idea that we were. (*The view inches forward.*)

Garvin: I'd say gettin' crushed by a fallin' body will do you in nice. (*The gun raises at the camera.*) But just in case-" (*Two shots ring out, the camera violently jerks backward and is then looking at the ceiling.*)

Garvin: (*Off camera*) Aw, that was too easy (*A gun comes into view, then there is a quick cutting motion, lots of movement and the camera is looking at Garvin standing up. It watches as the black knife goes into Garvin's body, then immediately is removed.)*

Mr. Blue: Really, Claude? You just said it. 'Too easy.' But you know what? People- they are easy to kill- as you will soon discover. But ideas? Oh, those are rather infinite. You might say that there is a whole…Host…of ways for the idea of me to live on.

Garvin: So you are just a copycat, just someone lookin' for a bit of fame. (*Garvin is backing up.*)

Mr. Blue: Now, now, let's not get hypocritical, Claude Garvin, haven't you enjoyed the limelight a bit of late?

Garvin: Screw you!" (*Garvin rushes with something in his hand, but the camera moves quickly and a knife sails through the air, hitting Garvin in the chest. He falls to the stairs, gasping.*)

(*The camera moves forward, then stops. It turns, looking backward. It sees a gun, the gun Mr. Blue had, it goes and retrieves it.*)

Mr. Blue: I don't think copycat is the right word, either. I prefer the term…evolution.(*The camera goes black, but the audio still picks up the following.*) And I am now so much more. Soon, everyone will learn that.

The sound went the way of the video, and the episode ended.

CHAPTER 16

It was one of those slow-motion moments for Knox. He pulled into his driveway, seeing the lights on inside, and jumped from the truck. He could see Claude's behemoth of a lifted truck in front of the house, but the scene was eerily quiet.

The front door was locked, so he fumbled with his keys and finally found the keyhole. The deadbolt thudded back, and the door swung open.

Knox could smell fresh vegetables and the scent of a candle burning somewhere nearby. Lindsey always had a fall scented candle going, even if it was the peak of summer.

But Knox also smelled something else. Something sweet, yet sick. His eye ran across the back of the house, where he could just barely see the edge of the kitchen but had a full view of the back door. And his heart sank. The door was shattered, and glass was strewn about the floor. His eyes noticed small red spots on the floor and followed them back toward himself. He walked along the wall of the entryway, drawing his gun and preparing for some horror behind the half-wall just ahead.

He took the corner and then gasped. Claude Garvin was lying there, his throat cut and several stab wounds in his chest. Knox wanted to scream for his family, but he didn't know if the killer of his former deputy- his *friend*- was still there. He cleared the area behind him and around the kitchen and then began to make his way up the stairs.

It was still dark, just as it had been when Cade Faust had made his ascent just minutes before. The difference was that Knox knew the house, and he knew where his family would hide. And he knew where an intruder might lay an ambush.

He checked the hall closets, the guest bedroom and Amber's room. He cleared the bathroom. He noticed that there was a trail of blood there, also, as well as broken picture frames down the hall. He fought the rising fear that was gripping his chest, making it difficult to breathe, and pressed forward.

The blood trail went into the bedroom, and sure enough, it went to the closet. Where Knox had taught them to hide. Blood had pooled there, and now tears stung Knox's eyes. Slowly, cautiously, and fearfully, he opened the closet.

Dr. Van Crewe lay in a pool of his own blood, but he was alone. No sign of Lindsey or Amber. Knox knelt down and checked his pulse- it was weak, but there was one. Knox pulled his phone from his pocket and called the dispatch number. He gave them his name and address and said, "I need an ambulance and a coroner here fast. There's been another murder...and I think a kidnapping."

The dispatcher asked how he knew that.

Knox rose and looked around the room, then froze. Written in blood on the wall behind his bed it said, "I have the writer, the cop, and the final girl. Come be the sacrifice, Knox."

"He left a note," Knox said grimly into the phone.

◆ ◆ ◆

Amber couldn't tell where they had gone, but the van had come to a stop. The light had grown even darker, leading her to think they had parked inside something. The door slid open, and she heard Mr. Blue say, "Welcome to the next round, ladies. Follow me. Actually, I'll follow you, heh, heh." He pulled them from the van and put what felt like knives at their backs, and prodded them forward. They walked up some steps, down a hall, then up more steps. Amber recognized the smell of the place they were in but couldn't place it. "Our fellow participants are waiting on us," Mr. Blue said, stopping them before a door and reaching between them to open it. He nudged them forth again, and said, "Easy now, the steps are steep."

Amber's foot found the step and the feel of

movement was familiar because she did it several times a week. She was in Professor Newman's classroom.

A mechanical voice came from the front of the room, on the stage where the professor normally stood. "You're late, clown," it said, almost whisper-like.

"There were...complications," Blue responded. "But I'm here now, and if you'll keep an eye on them, I have that complication in the car. Besides- *he's* not here yet."

Amber was shoved down into a chair, and then her hands were clasped behind her and once again fastened so she couldn't get free. Her feet were then latched in. She heard the same clasping noises next to her as her mother was 'seated.'

"Be right back!" Mr. Blue said, then she heard him mount the steps and leave the room.

The other voice didn't speak again, but in the silence, Amber could hear breathing.

Several people breathing, actually.

Blue was gone a short time, then when he returned, he went to the seat on the other side of Amber and set someone in it. More fastening in place, then Blue danced around in front of Amber and went to the far end of the stage. She heard him take a seat on a chair like her own, then another voice came from that side of the stage.

"Welcome, guests, to the event that all good true crime stories need," came the voice that Amber recognized instantly.

The Host.

Someone moved next to her, by her mother, and she heard what sounded like her mother's blindfold being removed.

Her mother screamed.

Then Amber's mask came off.

At first, a bright light from in front of her blinded her, and she blinked against its offending glare. As her eyes came into focus, she looked to her mother and saw terror in her eyes. "Amber, look at them!" she said in a panic.

Turning to look at her left, she saw that the newest prisoner was still wearing a bag over their head, but she felt sure it was Detective Faust. She had heard him in the altercation with Blue at the house, so she guessed it was him. Then she turned back toward her mother, and she screamed.

The Wraith.

The Brute.

The Pyro.

Mr. Blue.

All seated in a neat row staring out at the seats.

No.

Staring at the camera.

The camera that an unconscious Rogan Benson was leaning against.

Finally, the Host finished their introduction. "Welcome to the Reunion Episode!"

❖ ❖ ❖

"Sully, what happened?" Detective Joel yelled as he ran across the well-maintained lawn. Ambulance and police lights splashed across the front of the pale brick home and the EMTs rolled a semi-conscious Van Crewe to the waiting ambulance. A handful of uniformed officers were scrambling about, but so many others were scattered around the city dealing with the three other sets of murders and trying desperately to get ahead of the Host.

Knox was sitting on his front step, head in hands. The coroner had still not arrived for Claude, and Knox couldn't bear to be in the house with his body. He didn't hear Joel's question, he was thinking about how he had failed.

Again.

"Sully, I said, what happened?"

He looked up and realized that Joel was standing right there. "Joshua. Didn't see you." Knox looked out into space again, and was silent for a moment. Just as Joel was about to ask again, Knox spoke. "I wasn't here, Joshua. Claude was, like I asked him to be. I never gave him credit, not like he deserved. I just saw a blowhard redneck, but he was good. *Good*, you know. He died trying to protect my family."

"Where are they, Sully?" Knox asked gently, but urgently.

Knox shrugged and absently shook his head. "No idea. Crewe wasn't conscious enough to say much, and I doubt he'd know. Not like the Host would say where he was going."

Joel looked at him but said nothing. Then he climbed up the step and went inside the house.

Knox was spiraling. He knew he had to catch hold of himself because he was useless to everyone if he just gave up. But in his mind, the pieces of the puzzle buzzed around like moths at a lightbulb. One would strike a chord, then bounce uselessly away. He knew that at the heart of everything this Host was doing was the theme of secrets. Every target had a secret. But what secret could Lindsey or Amber have? Ambers was the documentary- what was Lindsey hiding? Why was Crewe at his house? Why hadn't Faust made it in time?

"Knox- come here, quick," Joel shouted.

Slowly, Knox rose and walked inside. There was Joel standing over Claude. The blood was growing dark around the body, pooling and flowing out in a nice, symmetrical pattern. Except for a streak by Claude's hand.

"Notice anything strange about the streak there?" Joel asked.

Knox shrugged again, his brain overwhelmed. His eyes followed the streak back to Claude's hand, untouched by the blood. Except...

"Is that blood on his finger?" Knox asked.

Joel knelt down. Without touching the body, he positioned himself to look closer. "It is. You think he made the streak with his finger? Why would he?"

Knox felt a moth land on the lightbulb. It stayed there this time. His eyes went to the pool of blood and saw a small flaw in the perfect circle. Like someone touched it. He thought at first it could have been the killer, with the message he left upstairs. But the moth was still on the lightbulb.

"It's not a streak," Knox said. "It's a one."

Joel looked closer. "It is. Why?"

Knox was finding traction again. "We have Nikki Meyers and Pastor Casey- both dead. The FBI agents slaughtered- what was the secret there? And the fire- where was that?"

"The professor's house," Joel replied. "Wagglin. Why?"

"None of these have happened at the same time? None of the murders?" Knox asked.

Joel thought a moment. "No, at least ten minutes between each attack."

"Was the professor killed?"

Joel shook his head. "No."

"Know where he is?"

"No."

"Claude and I had a prime suspect. Newman," Knox said. "That 'one' could mean Claude identified Newman."

Joel looked at Knox. "Or? There seemed like there was another alternative."

Knox bit his lip and sighed. "Or there is just one killer out on the town tonight."

♦ ♦ ♦

"Wake up, sleepy heads," the Host shouted.

Amber watched as the row of killers began to shift in their seats, but not rise. Rogan also woke, and when he saw Amber, he shouted, "Hey- let her go! She's not part of this!"

"Rogan- are you part of it?" Amber yelled back, her voice breaking.

"He is, dear," the Host said, pointing a gun at Rogan, who dutifully manned the camera. "He's telling our story. Yours, theirs-" he gestured toward the killers- "and mine. Most importantly, mine, of course. Telling it right. As it was meant to be. And telling it live!"

Amber looked back toward Rogan and saw that several computers surrounded the camera. She noticed that cameras were on either side of the stage, too. All were running.

The Host moved to center stage and faced Rogan's camera. "As my fans are tuning in, let me just catch you up on the evening's festivities. Killtown was almost three years ago, and while it was a good time, it was ultimately a failure. The contestants all fell. Because I believe that they were not properly trained. Properly educated in the spilling of blood. So, this very night I have hosted Kill U- a night for new killers to test their skills. We have the Wraith, the Brute, the Pyro, and Mr. Blue. We have me. Our friend the Novice is running a bit behind- he will join us soon enough. And, because in the original Killtown, we had a Hero- Tommy Hanover- we have our own version. Detective Cade Faust. The man who killed the original Novice and officially ended Killtown!" He pointed a black gloved finger at the hooded figure next to Amber.

"Why are we here?" Lindsey yelled. Faust began to struggle with his bonds.

The Host turned slowly, glaring with those cracked, red eyes. "In good time, Lindsey Knox." He turned back to face the camera. "Yes, that is Lindsey Knox, author of Killtown. And she is not here because she survived the first Killtown. No, no, no. She is here because she has a secret. A secret she discovered when writing her little book. One she didn't tell *anyone*. Well, almost no one. Someone had to find out, because *I* found out. And tonight, secrets will be revealed! But first, let me also introduce our cameraman…"

Amber leaned over to her mother. "What secret?"

Lindsey was ashen, and she didn't look at Amber. "It can't be that…why would that make a difference to anything?" She seemed to be talking to herself.

"Mom- what? What did you find?"

Finally, Lindsey turned to Amber. "I found a connection. It- it was so ridiculous I didn't put it in the book because I thought no one would believe it. And no one *needed* to know that-"

A gunshot rang out and Lindsey lurched backward.

Amber screamed as blood sprayed across her face.

Lindsey yelled out, and a small red circle on her shoulder grew larger and larger.

The Host rushed over and pulled her chair back up. "No spoilers- save it for the big reveal. Or next time, it goes right here-" he tapped her forehead. "Now, viewers, make your guesses. What was the big secret? Share in the message boards. And while we wait, let me tell you why Nikki Meyers had to die tonight..."

CHAPTER 17

"I guess Faust made it here after all," Knox commented as he looked at the shattered pictures in his upstairs hallway. Beneath the glass was a badge, and Joel confirmed it was his partner's.

"Looks like he was taken by the killer, but why? What does Cade Faust have to do with this?" Joel asked. "Decorated cop, rookie detective-"

"Don't forget- he has ties to Killtown, too," Knox interrupted. "He killed Densman. He's a... hero..." Knox trailed off.

"What?"

"Everyone knows the villains of Killtown," Knox explained. "But there was one guy- Tommy Hanover. He was one of the people that had been invited. He wanted to kill the killers and be a hero. He was called "the Hero" in the chats they dug up. A war vet whose PTS made him violent, so he wanted to channel that into something good. Warped, but good."

"So?"

"So, Hanover never killed anyone," Knox said. "He died trying to rescue some others- who turned out to be the actual Hosts. The kills tonight have mirrored some kills in Killtown. Pastor Casey was like Bob Atkins- but Casey didn't kill his killer. The Pyro blew up a firetruck- because he was killed by the one Claude was driving. And here...Lindsey was taken in Kingston. By the clown. Maybe he took Faust to play out the role of Hero- to die trying to save someone. A sacrifice."

Joel looked at Knox and blinked. "You know you started calling it 'Killtown?' Didn't you have a hangup about that?"

Knox grimaced. "Got a lot more important things to worry about than my issues with a word. That, or therapy finally worked."

"Detective!" A uniformed officer ran up the stairs and handed Joel a tablet. "This started streaming everywhere about five minutes ago."

Knox looked over Joel's shoulder and felt his heart sink. He saw Lindsey and Amber tied to chairs in a room that was oddly familiar yet effectively disguised. And Lindsey was bleeding. But the focus was on that wooden masked madman. Explaining why Nikki Meyers had to die. The room really looked familiar- why was that? Then he saw something else in the background. "Joshua, look!"

The killers of Killtown were seated on the stage behind the Host. "Can you tell where they are?" Joel asked.

But Sullivan Knox was already gone.

❖ ❖ ❖

"You see, Nikki Meyers was an awful, awful person," the Host was explaining. "Not only did she hate *my* story, but she actively sought to quiet Rogan Benson's freedom to speak, because it offended her. And was she a sainted woman? Oh, she would have had you believe that, but she was engaged in an affair with the president of King University, Holden Straub. Who also had to die because he was stealing- *stealing-* from the university. Raising tuition to cover his own lavish lifestyle. These two, they are archetypes of societal rot. The deep pocketed greed and the condescending hypocrisy that holds *all* the power. We, the little people, are power*less* in their midst. We can simply watch as they build their empires on *our* hard work, blood, sweat, and tears. But no more."

Amber was watching as the Host launched into a hard sell, a persuasion to join his cause, if you could call it that. Her attention turned to her mother, who was sweating and grinding her teeth in pain. "Mom, are you okay?"

"It hurts, but I think the fall may have loosened my bonds a bit," Lindsey said.

Amber looked at her mother in awe. She was wounded, but still fighting. That was when she realized something was off with the whole situation. She looked down at the row of killers. Just sitting there, not moving. No, that wasn't right. They were moving, but all of them wore black robes. The movement was beneath the robe...and was very similar to her mother's struggles against her bonds.

"Now, another archetype of detritus, organized religion," the Host transitioned, and began walking toward the Wraith. "Pastor Felix Casey was a lap dog of Nikki Meyer, and a beacon of hate and judgment- while holding his own little secret. Wraith, take it away."

Without moving, the Wraith began to speak. "Pastor Casey was in possession of copious amounts of child pornography," the Wraith said in his whisper voice. He then began to detail how Casey was killed.

Amber noted that the Wraith had a small, green light on a small piece of black plastic just below his chin. Looking at each killer, she saw they all had the same device, but their lights were a steady red. All except for the Brute, who had nothing. The green light blinked when the Wraith spoke, but then when he stopped and the Host began to talk, the light went red.

The Pyro was talking then, explaining why he targeted Professor Newman. "He was having an affair with a student, Margot Lucas. I set his home ablaze like his passion set his career and his morality aflame. The powerful taking advantage of the weak once again."

Amber looked to Rogan, who looked terrified, but he kept filming. He was mouthing something to her, but she couldn't make it out. It looked like he was saying, "Friends."

"Now, Brute, tell us about the cops you killed-" the Host was asking, standing by the Brute. "Wait- you can't. You don't talk. But I was there, had to pick up my camera operator. See, the feds he killed were merely collateral damage. His real target was Senator Saul King. That's right, the star legislator from Texas. Sadly, Senator King was able to survive the attack, and he has his own secrets, too. But that will also have to wait a bit. Mr. Blue?"

The voice of the clown began to resonate in the room, and he explained that he was tasked with acquiring Lindsey Knox. "You see, she wrote Killtown's story, but omitted some very important, very integral facts about one of the participants. Things that might turn the whole story on its head. Now, Host, I believe you want to finish the story?"

"Thank you Mr. Blue," the Host mock bowed and turned back to the camera. "First, you need to know that the Killtown contestants engaged in something that no one- not even those who witnessed it recognized. Sean Densman, the Novice, was a sacrifice. Well, he was supposed to be. All of the killers attacked him. Amber-" the Host turned toward her and nearly sprinted to her. "You saw it- on the football field. You screamed, and they left him. But what you didn't know- heh- what even Sean didn't know was that he had a genetic condition. The same one the Brute had. Congenital insensitivity to pain. He couldn't feel pain. Your scream and his condition saved him. For a time. But that's not Lindsey Knox's secret. See, she decided that no one needed to know that Sean had a brother. That they were separated in this state's horrific foster care system with biological parents whose identities *she* never knew. She never told anyone because she feared the surviving brother wouldn't be able to deal with what Sean had done." The Host paused, then looked at Lindsey. "Or what the brother had done to Sean."

"No," Lindsey whispered.

"Looks like the Novice has arrived," the Host announced. He whipped off his mask and revealed the black ski mask. Looking out of those eye holes were dead, brown eyes. "And since this Hero killed the Novice the first time, let's turn the tables!" He spun and lifted a shotgun he had hidden under his cloak, firing once into Cade Faust's head, and his body flew back and was still. "That felt good!" the Host shouted.

Amber screamed.

Lindsey finally freed her hands and feet and rushed the Host. She hit him and knocked the gun from his hand, and the two of them tumbled toward the front row of desks. He kicked her off of him, and rose, pulling two knives from his belt.

"Yes, Lindsey, let's set the record straight."

Lindsey was backing away when the back door burst open and Sully charged in. He fired twice at the Host, the first hitting his shoulder and the second missing. The Host rushed the stage and snatched up the wooden mask. There was a buzzing noise and all of the killers suddenly rose from their seats and began looking around.

As the Host fled the room, the lights went out.

CHAPTER 18

In the darkness, Knox could still see people moving. Low emergency lights came on, giving a haunting view to the room. He saw Rogan Benson seated- no strapped down- to a chair behind the various cameras, and he went to free him, keeping a wary eye on the risen killers.

If that is who they were.

Rogan's eyes were wide and he screamed, "STOP!"

Knox turned and saw that Lindsey had grabbed the shotgun and was drawing a bead on the clown, who was waving their hands frantically. His wife turned to look up and Rogan yelled, "They aren't the killers!"

Knox watched as the figures removed the masks they were wearing to reveal Amber's friends. The clown was Asher, the Brute was Dex. Mikey was the Wraith, and Liv was the Pyro. All of them had duct tape over their mouths, which they attempted- unsuccessfully- to gingerly remove with much protestation. Knox noted that each of them had a dull, steel ring around their neck.

Turning back to his most pressing task,

Knox pulled his pocket knife out and cut Rogan's bonds, then helped him to his feet. "Thanks, Mr. Knox. He had me filming everything."

Knox looked at Rogan with suspicion. Could he trust the kid's word? Maybe he was in on it after all? "Is it really Faust?"

"No idea," Rogan said. "He always had the mask on."

"It was Faust," Dex said. "He came and got us, said it was for protective custody. Once he got us in the car, he gassed us with something. When we woke up, we were here, locked into those chairs."

"He used some sort of speaker," Liv said. "He would talk but the sound would come from us, sounding like the killers."

"He had a computer, too," Mikey said. "He was controlling something. I think he was running some sort of AI to make calls for him as the Host."

Asher was silent, but he nodded.

Knox looked them over. It was a lot to take in, for sure. He turned back to Rogan. "How much did you see? At my house, when he went there?"

Rogan shook his head. "I wasn't there. He used a body cam for that. It streamed straight from source."

"To where?"

Rogan sighed. "Followers. People who were following my podcast. They got wrapped up in his story, and somehow he found them. Radicalized them...made them a...cult."

Amber screamed, and Knox turned and raced down the steps toward her, but he slowed his pace when he saw why she screamed. The body laying on the floor was not Faust. It was Margot Lucas. They had pulled the mask off, and her blonde hair fell on the floor and into the pool of blood that surrounded her ruined face.

Knox took Amber into his arms, and she buried her face in his chest. Lindsey, shock washing over her face, ran to him as well. They embraced as a family while the others stared at their dead friend in abject horror.

"Wellllll, now isn't that interesting?" came the voice of Mr. Blue, piped in through the sound system. Then the voice shifted to a mechanical whisper- the Wraith. "Where is Detective Faust? Perhaps not all is as it seems." Then the muffled voice of the Pyro added, "And what about Professor Newman? Did he just barely escape the flames..." Finally, the Host chimed in. "Or was the man behind it all along?"

"We gotta get outta here," Liv said, frantically looking all around for an escape. "I can't stay here!" And with that, she sprinted up the steps and ran for the door. She brushed past Rogan and took the steps two by two. She burst through the door-

And her head exploded in flame.

Her body fell back into the room, smoke and cinder wafting up from her neck as the anguished voice of the Pyro wailed over the speakers.

There was a moment's pause, then each of the people with the metal rings around their neck began to pull at the deadly accessory with frantic terror.

"Ah...one down..." the Host said over the loudspeaker. "You see, it has gotten a little too crowded in here, and I brought you all here to... free up some space. Each of you...killers... has a special little necklace, designed based on who you are a proxy for. Liv was the Pyro- rest her soul- and she died by fire. Now, I do not want to spoil the surprise, but if you don't follow my rules, then you will each meet a unique and creative end."

Knox looked back at Rogan and whispered, "Where is he? Does he have cameras?"

Rogan nodded in affirmative, then nodded at the office behind the stage. Newman's office. Knox knew there were two missing variables- Cade Faust and Bennett Newman. One- or both- were probably the Host. And they probably were in that room. He didn't know why, but the motive could wait. It was about survival and stopping the rampage. But if the killer was telling the truth, then survival was not as simple as just avoiding the Host. Knox took Rogan by the shoulders and looked him in the eyes. "Find that feed- I bet he's live streaming now. It's his big climax, but if we can see what he sees, we might be able to stay ahead of him. Can you find it?"

Rogan looked from Knox to his friends to

the headless body of Liv before Knox shook him and he turned back. His eyes were cloudy, his gaze unfocused, but he said, "Yeah. I think so."

"Get to it, then. I'm gonna check the office," Knox said, turning to face Lindsey and Amber, who were huddled together in an embrace. The other three were shouting and pulling at their steel rings, but he knew there was nothing he could do about that now. He pulled out his phone and texted Detective Joel what they knew. That they suspected Faust. No sense in wasting Joel's considerable talents. If there was more to come, it might not be just in that room. The Host had shown a proficiency with intricate traps and technology, so it was conceivable that much more mayhem was on deck.

Turning to his family, he paused. Why them? Why did this have to keep happening for them? He swore he would do all he could to end it that night. "Amber," he said, gently placing a hand on his daughter's shoulder. "Is there a door out of the office? The one in front of the class?"

"No, it's just a room."

"Got the feed!" Rogan shouted. "But it's just dark now."

Knox looked at the door. It was a trap, he was sure of it. Why else would the Host hide in a room with one way in and no way out? He checked his gun, then started to walk toward the door. As he did, his foot kicked the shotgun lying on the floor. He knelt down and picked it up, then turned to Lindsey and handed it to her. "If he gets past me, take him out. Then run."

He started for the door, gun at the ready. He placed his hand on the door and raised his weapon to prepare for an attack. Then he flung the door open.

Immediately, two voices began to yell at him. To his left, Faust was tied to a chair and shouting, "Shoot him- it's Newman!"

To his right, Bennett Newman was also tied up, shouting, "He burned my house and tried to kill me!"

Knox looked from man to man, trying to process what to do. In the split second he had, he evaluated that one of these men was pretending to be held captive, and the other was the Host. But how to tell?

From the auditorium, Rogan yelled, "The camera is filming you on your right!"

Without hesitation, Knox shot Newman in the head.

The room went silent as the body slumped in the chair. Knox breathed deeply, then walked over to untie Faust. He kept his gun in one hand as he bent down to loosen whatever bonds held the detective, just in case.

"Should've guessed I'd want to play a little game, Knox," Faust whispered. Then Knox was struck in the abdomen by two fists. He stumbled back, dropping the pistol, and he looked down. Blood was pouring from his stomach. He looked up and saw Faust standing, pulling the mask of the Host onto his face. "I'm not just a man of many talents," he said, the voice of the Host taking over midway through the sentence. "I've got a host of personalities rattling around in here, too."

◆ ◆ ◆

s apartment when Knox's text came in. "Great minds think alike," he muttered to himself. His cruiser pulled onto the curb outside his partner's residence, and behind him was a SWAT van with four officers dressed for combat. Getting out his car, Joel slipped on his flak jacket and addressed the SWAT guys. "No idea what to expect in there. He could be holed up and waiting, he could be nowhere near here. He was one of us, he knows our tactics. Be ready."

They went up the sidewalk single file, Joel in the rear. At the door, the lead officer yelled, "Open up, Faust! Police?"

After a beat, he kicked the door in. The SWAT team entered and fanned out, covering the room. Within thirty seconds, they announced, "Clear!"

Joel went in.

He had never been to his partner's apartment. Not surprising since they had just been teamed up. It was dark. Chaotic. There seemed to be different sections of the room devoted to the killers of Killtown. Almost like shrines. He had gotten crimes scene photos of all the killers, and they had been blown up, the headshots, like some macabre religious iconography.

The largest shrine had a four foot tall wooden carving of the Host mask as the background. Several wooden masks, slightly different in appearance to the real mask but clear attempts at imitation, were scattered on a workbench that was attached to the mask backdrop. And nailed that backdrop was a picture of Cade Faust. Joel approached it, and as he got closer, he realized it wasn't Cade. It was Sean Densman. The Novice.

Joel had noticed the similarity before, but looking at Densman's old picture in that moment, it was uncanny. Like they were...

"Identical twins..." he said in a whisper.

"Detective, you wanna look over here?"

Joel pulled himself away from the image, his mind reeling at the implications that his partner was the identical twin of a serial killer wannabe. The SWAT officer directed him to a computer console- array was a better word. Five screens and CPUs, numerous recording devices, voice modulators, and the remnants of gadgets Cade must have been building.

"Was it Cade all along?" the officer asked.

Joel wondered about that, too. Faust had been there when the killer called, interacted with the killer, even. How could that be? Unless...

"Chatbots," Joel said.

"Sir?"

"He was running some AI software that would call us, make it look like the Host was calling, but it was this setup," Joel said. "He created the image of multiple killers using this technology, but it was just him. All along, it was just him."

"Good call, partner!"

A small, sixth screen had sparked to life. The face of the Host filled the screen. His mocking voice continued. "But you don't have it all. Not yet. I don't think you'll ever figure out all that is going on in my head!"

"Is this really you, or one of your AI simulations?" Joel asked.

"Oh, it's me. Live and uncut," the Host replied. He shifted the camera view to show a bloody and semi-conscious Sullivan Knox laying in a darkening red pool. "And I've got work to do. So, to my fans, to my followers, the time is now to judge our corrupt police officers. Those who wield such power with so little responsibility. Why, Detective Joel here was partnered with a serial killer, and never even tried to stop me!"

"How could I know, Cade?" Joel shouted.

"Oh, dear detective," the Host chided. "I was never Cade- I was always Sean Densman. Perhaps it is not corruption that I punish you for, but incompetence. Goodbye!"

The screen blinked off, and Joel heard a click. He had just a moment to recognize the sight of

C-4 strapped under the computer console, and to shove the SWAT officer as far away as he could before the explosion ripped apart the computer array and Detective Joshua Joel.

◆ ◆ ◆

Amber watched in horror as her father emerged from the office being held up by the Host. She could see the blood-soaked front of his shirt and the paleness of his face. His head lolled to the side and she knew he was in bad shape. And now, the Host was using him as a human shield.

Lindsey trained the shotgun on him, and she said, "Let him go, now!" Amber heard her mother's voice break, but she also heard strength underlying her terror.

Amber also saw Asher and Dex moving into position behind the Host while Mikey was coming up on his right. The killer didn't seem to see them.

"Now, Lindsey, why would I do that?" the Host asked. "It would make me so vulnerable. So *weak*. Isn't that what you called me, Lindsey? *Weak*?"

"Faust, I never called you weak," Lindsey said. "I never even mentioned you in the book. I didn't want to be the one to tell you your brother was a murderer and the man you killed that day outside Kingston. Not in a book. Not like that."

The Host laughed. It echoed behind

the mask, but since he was still linked into the auditorium sound system and Rogan was streaming the video, it sounded like there were dozens of him.

"Lindsey, Lindsey, Lindsey. So close, yet so far. I did kill my brother that day. And I knew it." The Host paused, grew very still, then said, "But it was Cade Faust that died that day, not Sean Densman." He pushed Knox away and drew a pistol- Knox's gun- and shot Lindsey. The mask must have messed with his aim, as it struck her on the other shoulder instead of her heart, and she fell backward, dropping the gun. Amber rushed to her mother's side, screaming.

"Now!" Dex yelled as he jumped on the Host, joined by Asher and Mikey. But he was ready for them. He slashed Asher across the chest, pushing him back, and fired wildly at Mikey. She dodged and fell to the floor, and then Dex grabbed him, wrapping his arms around his chest. Amber watched as the Host threw his head back and collided with Dex's forehead. He held on anyway, and shifted his body weight, throwing the Host into the first row of chairs.

The gun clattered to the floor, as did a small remote. Mikey dove for both, but missed the gun, which spun farther away upon her making contact. She flipped it around in her hand, then shouted, "I think I got the neck things figured out!" She pressed a button and sure enough, they unclasped and fell from their necks.

Amber looked over her mother and saw she was breathing, but slipping out of consciousness. Lindsey looked at her and mouthed, "Go."

Amber shook her head and tried to put pressure on the wound. Lindsey took her daughter's hand and pushed it away. She said aloud, "Go. I'll be fine." She gave a wink, then her eyes closed.

"Mom!" Amber yelled, and a commotion broke out behind her.

Asher, clutching the shallow wound on his chest turned to Amber and yelled, "Run! We'll hold him!"

Rogan ran to Amber and pulled her away from her mother. "He's right- he wants you now. We need to go get help!"

Amber turned and saw Dex land a punch to the back of the Host's head, and he fell to the ground. She glimpsed the killer's hand close around the knife hilt in his belt. Dex yelled, "Go-NOW!"

Amber ran with Rogan for the door.

She scooped up the shotgun as she ran. She had a feeling she might still need it.

CHAPTER 19

He felt their blows landing on his back and smiled behind his mask. It did not hurt him, after all.

He remembered other times when the blows fell upon him. In the Densman home at the hands of his foster parents who later adopted him. They took him in not out of love, but out of financial need. His 'father' used fists more effectively than he used words and was always frustrated when Sean didn't seem bothered by the beatings. Even when they resulted in trips to the ER.

He was beaten in juvie, too. Bigger kids, or the gangs that formed out of survival instinct would target him. In fact, the only safe place he had ever found was in the State Hospital, when his doctor finally got him admitted.

It was there that he learned about his unique condition. Not the 'unable to feel pain' thing. No, that he knew.

Sean learned about dissociative identity disorder.

His doctor told him that trauma was often

a factor in the disorder's development. That the person often created unique personalities as protectors, as the characters who had the strength to do what they could not. Sean knew nothing of this, because he would just black out and find himself in a new situation. Usually, one where he had just hurt someone.

It was also in the hospital that Sean learned the personality that took over was his adoptive father.

His doctor taught Sean coping skills, and he learned to control the transition. Then Sean wondered if he might be able to kill the other personality. Symbolically, of course, but to take the life out of his intellectual hijacker.

When he took his first actual life, during Killtown, it was not his victim's face he saw- it was his foster father's.

And the voice went silent.

Then, that same night, his supposed friends struck him down. They claimed it was a 'sacrifice' to Killtown, but Sean knew what it really was.

He was their scapegoat.

But they didn't know about Sean's lack of pain sensitivity.

Or what happened when someone hurt him.

The abuser became a part of his psyche.

He became his own abuser.

Sean Densman was the Pyro.

Sean Densman was the Wraith.

Sean Densman was the Brute.

Sean Densman was Mr. Blue.

Sean Densman was the Host.

And he really was. That night, Killtown, he became the host of all those killers. They became ghosts in his machine, separate identities that would steal his consciousness from him in moments of stress. It would normally take some time for these identities to manifest, but then something else happened to Sean.

His very own brother tried to arrest him.

To kill him.

Sean knew all about Cade Faust, how he had been adopted by the good family, how he turned out to be a *good* son. When Sean looked out from behind the mask of the Host and saw his own face, he knew. Fate had brought them together.

At first, his plan was to carry on the ruse long enough to escape.

Then something happened.

In the struggle, the voices whispered a bigger plan to Sean. A plan that would not just save him, but also ruin the brother who got the life that should have been Sean's.

Now, mixed in with the Killtown killers, was Cade Faust. With all his goodness, all his honor. For the first time in his life, Sean was getting positive praise. And slowly, Cade took over.

His psychiatrist was the same one that got him into the state hospital. Of course, 'Cade' never recognized him, but Sean did. The doctor spoke often of Cade embracing his trauma, learning to live his new life and make the best of it. Sean/Host, sitting just below the surface took that advice to heart.

And so Sean became Cade, and Cade did very well.

Until that podcast.

Then Killtown came back, and Cade started to black out. He had gaps in his memory, lost time. During those times, the Host took over- or Mr. Blue or one of the others. But Cade never knew. Never suspected. Somehow, he just never saw that all his research on Killtown was just feeding the hidden identities, strengthening them.

And Sean, who had melded with the Host so that the two were almost indistinguishable, began to plan a way to take over once more.

He had reached the point where he was ready to be rid of them all.

Save one.

The Host.

His hand curled around the hilt of the knife in his belt. The athlete- the one who was the Brute when Sean looked at him- yelled, "Go- NOW!" to Amber. The final girl. The true sacrifice the Host demanded. She and the podcaster ran, but he wasn't worried. He knew they wouldn't get far before he caught up to them.

Sean pulled the knife and swung his arm to the side, driving the blade into the basketball star's ankle. He felt the blade strike bone and the weight of the man fall on his back. Sean shrugged him off, then turned to the funny one. He saw Mr. Blue, despite it being Asher.

Asher, who was in love with a girl who would never return his affection. Asher, who held his hand to his bleeding chest and pronounced with false bravado, "You can't take us all, mother-"

Swift as lightning, Sean was in Mr. Blue's face, and the knife slashed across his open mouth. Blood sprayed into the wooden mask, a sort of dark baptism, as Sean once again felt the Host taking over. Not that they were all that different, not anymore. Sean was the Host, and the Host was Sean. All the other voices were going quiet. But just then, Mr. Blue was pleading for his life.

So the Host slit his throat.

As he gurgled the life from his body, the Host relentless kept stabbing him in the chest, over and over. The cackling laughter in Sean's head grew quieter with each blow.

Mr. Blue collapsed into a pile of Asher Hunter and a pool of blood- then grew silent.

Mikey was trying to get away, but Sean saw only the black clad Wraith taking the same route Amber and Rogan had taken. He went after them, but a hand grabbed his foot. He turned to see the Brute on the floor, then felt his balance shift and he went down. The Brute rose, and stood over Sean. The Brute was looking around, and Sean knew he was trying to find the gun. The Host pulled his legs to his chest, then launched his feet into the Brute's chest. He didn't fall, but the Host was on his feet and holding both the silver knife and the black knife. Like a boxer doing a bag workout, he began to pummel the Brute's midsection, the knives eviscerating the Brute. Cutting away the mass and muscle of the beast and leaving only Dex Smalley's lifeless body.

The Host crossed his arms and wiped the bloody blades off on his biceps, then turned to pursue the Wraith. His black cape and hood were covered in blood and viscera.

It had been the Wraith's betrayal that hurt the worst that night. The Wraith had actually tried to teach Sean. Sean had begun to think he might had actually found a friend and mentor for the first time since he left the hospital.

But the Wraith's blade had cut deep. Deeper than the severed tissues in his back would indicate. It was this single-minded revenge that drove the Host from the room without confirming Knox or Lindsey were dead. They no longer mattered. There was only the cleansing of his mind and the death of the girl. For Killtown. For Kill U.

For the future.

For the Host.

He saw the Wraith run down the stairs just as he emerged from the doors of the auditorium. He noticed they were moving slowly, but it did not connect that Mikey had sprained her ankle in her fall, because he did not see Mikey Brooks.

Just the Wraith.

He ran over to the floor to ceiling window that looked out on the courtyard and waited. The Wraith came into view below him, and so the Host backed up and sprinted into the window. It shattered all around him as he sailed out and down toward the Wraith from the second floor.

The impact drove them both to the ground near a flower bed. Mikey had enough presence of mind to snatch fist-sized rock and try to use it as a weapon. She struck the Host across the face over and over, and finally the left red eye shattered. Small slivers of fiberglass tore into the flesh around Sean's eye, and into Sean's eye, but he felt no pain. The Host grabbed the hand with the rock and began to stab the Wraith over and over. He did not hear Mikey's death scream, he heard a gasping final whisper as the Wraith left his mind.

There was just Sean and the Host now.

And they were the same.

He turned and saw, in the distant night, two figures running. He began to pursue them.

As he sprinted, his mind went to the most outlandish and strange- yet completely true- part of Sean Densman's story. That his separated at birth, identical twin had been the man that arrived to arrest him after Killtown. Sean knew as soon as he saw Cade Faust who he was. It was why he donned the mask, to sustain that element of suspense.

It had also saved him. The buckshot from Cade's shotgun tore through the wooden mask and made hamburger of his face, but it stopped the pellets from penetrating into his skull. The beauty of the moment had been that Cade had no idea who Sean was.

That made the revelation so sweet.

See, Sean had found and kept up with Cade. Cade the golden boy who got the good home. Cade who got all the breaks, Cade who was bound to be a hero.

And that was a wound too deep for even Sean Densman to endure.

As the Host gained ground on his prey, his mind shifted back to that day three years earlier, when random chance had given him the chance to seal his destiny.

❖ ❖ ❖

Sean lost consciousness for a mere moment after the shotgun blast ripped through his mask. He could hear Cade moving around, checking on his dead partner, but the cracks in the red eyes made it very difficult to see clearly.

But he could feel his brother moving closer.

And we he got close enough, Sean would act.

"I have the suspect wounded and, on the ground," Cade was saying. Sean could feel that he was standing close enough. His hand snaked out toward Cade's feet. "Officer Camden is dead, but I can hold the susp-"

Sean rolled as Faust fell backward. The

shotgun stayed in the cop's hand, but hit the ground, stock first, which caused it to fire into the trees above. Sean was quick to rise to his feet, and he stood over Cade, mustering all the menace he could manage. Sean waited for Cade to look at him, because he wanted the moment to have a flare of drama. As his ignorant brother looked at the wooden mask, Sean slowly removed it.

Cade recoiled in shock, but there was no sign of recognition. Sean saw the thick blood covering the inside of the mask, and he knew his moment was ruined.

In a rage, Sean reached for the gun in his brother's hands.

Faust held the gun tightly, and rose to his feet as they struggled for control of the weapon. Sean was face-to-ruined-face with his brother, and the other man had no idea. Rage and adrenaline flooded his system, and with a surge of strength, Sean began getting the upper hand on Faust.

"Give...ugh..up, Sean," Faust grunted.

It might have been the mention of his name by his unknowing brother, or the blood loss, but something shifted in Sean's mind. He and Host merged into one. And that one was the Host. "There is no Sean. Only the Host remains. And a good host returns the gifts of their guests." With a swift twist, Sean pulled the shotgun down and fired the gun. He had twisted it enough that it only struck Cade, but just a bit more than a glancing blow.

The Host looked at Cade and saw that his nose was gone, as was much of his brow. Small holes in the upper lip showed teeth behind them, but there was a determination in Cade Faust's brown eyes that was familiar to the Host.

He had seen it in the mirror.

Cade kicked, and caught the Host in the shoulder, and the gun flew from his hands. It fell almost exactly equidistant between them.

Both men saw their moment, and went for the gun.

The Host got there first, but Cade still made a go of it. The Host pushed and kicked and freed the gun from Cade's grip. Cade rolled away, and put his hands up. "Okay, you win…just….just let me go."

The Host looked at Cade, confusion and rage tangled up in his ruined expression. "Let you go? Why would I do that? You're my ticket out of this."

"How?"

The Host chuckled. "You have no idea who I am. Who you are. We are brothers, separated at birth. You were raised by a good family. I got the dregs. We are identical- and what's more, that means our DNA is, too. I don't know if it was fate, or the Host himself who brought us together today, but only one of us is walking out. And that person will be me- as you."

"You're crazy!' Cade yelled.

The Host smiled. "Maybe, Cade. But I'm not

wrong."

"How do you know me?"

"Oh, I've followed you for some time," the Host said. "And while I didn't plan this, I've learned a lot about planning mayhem in the last twenty-four hours. It will take time, but I will become you, then I will ruin you. Because I can. Because I deserve to win. Then, I will teach others to be like me. To be the Host. To crush our enemies, to root out the detritus of humanity. All of it."

"You're crazy," Cade said once more.

The Host's smile vanished. "You said that once. I hate when people repeat themselves."

He blasted Cade Faust into oblivion.

He knew time was short, so he stripped Cade out of his uniform and put it on. Then he redressed Cade. He had no worries about DNA, because, why would he? As the sound of sirens drew nearer, the Host set the scene. Then, he laid down, and began his life as Cade Faust.

The hardest part had been doing the bland and boring police work and hiding his urges. Though Cade was the driving identity during that time, Sean/Host watched and waited, just out of consciousness. It took him months to recover, and a year of surgery. It never hurt, but he was in pain. He needed to kill. He shifted his focus into learning the personal habits of his brother, but living in another person's skin was easy. He had done it his whole life.

When the podcast started, Cade was listening, and thus, so was the Host. He began to work at controlling the switches, and while 'Cade' was researching Killtown as therapy, the Host was strengthening the personalities of the Pyro, the Brute, the Wraith, and Mr. Blue. And he got really good at controlling the switches between Sean, the Host, and Cade.

His skill as a criminal actually made him a good cop, and he rose rapidly in the smaller city's force. When he made detective, the Host knew the time was near. Even if Cade was oblivious.

The Host had, after all, spent much of his recovery building an online school of killers. A host of Hosts, as it were. He piggy-backed off of Rogan Benson's podcast, dropped morsels for the fans, and built a nearly deified persona for the Host. None would be actual killers, not until after the Host had fully returned. Oh, but they would be ready one day. Of that, the Host was sure.

School wasn't really the appropriate term for what the erstwhile Sean Densman built.

It was a cult.

And the Host was their god.

And now the time for the sacrifice was near.

CHAPTER 20

"He's gaining on us!"

Amber looked back as Rogan shouted his warning, and sure enough, the Host was sprinting toward them. Neither had their phones, so they had been trying to get into any building that might have a phone- that was why their pursuer had caught up. Now, they were near the edge of campus and the options were running out.

"What about the studio?" Amber asked breathlessly.

"Yes! I still have my keys!" Rogan said. They turned and ran straight to the building on their right. He fumbled with the keys, and Amber turned around and lifted the shotgun to a firing position. But the Host was nowhere in sight. Had they lost him?

Rogan cursed as he dropped the keys, then knelt to pick them up.

"Hurry, Rogan, I don't see him, but I know he's out there."

"I'm going as fast as I can," Rogan said, finally getting the lock to turn. "I'm in." He pushed the door open, and they ran in. They started to run up the stairs, but Rogan stopped on the second step. "Crap- I need to lock it!" He turned and ran back to the door.

"NO! We can lock him out of the studio!" Amber protested, but Rogan was already at the door. Reluctantly, she went back with him, seeing as she was the one with the gun.

But Rogan had stopped dead in his tracks. The door was wide open. They had definitely closed it. "Go. Now," Rogan said flatly.

They turned and ran up the stairs. When they reached the second floor, where the studio was, they could clearly hear heavy footfalls echoing through the otherwise silent hall. But they saw nothing.

Rogan ran to the door leading to the studio and went to unlock it. "Huh. It was already unlocked."

Amber ran up to him, frantic. "We have to go someplace else- it has to be a trap."

"I don't have keys to any other place- I'm sure I left it unlocked," Rogan said, opening the door. "Besides, he was downstairs, right?"

Amber stopped. Her eyes searched Rogan's face, looking for deception. Her gut told her something was off- or was she just so terrified that everyone and everything was to be doubted? "What if there are two?"

Rogan sighed. "C'mon, Amber, who else could it be? It's just the Host."

Amber took a step back. "It could be you,

Rogan. You spent how much time with him today? You being the sole survivor to tell the story would make your documentary a hit. How do I know you weren't working with him the whole time? Willingly?"

Rogan moved toward her, then stopped. "Amber, that's crazy. But I get it. You've been through this once before. So, you do what you need to do. But I'm going in here and calling the police." Then Rogan turned and went into the studio.

"You should have gone with him, Amber."

She spun around and saw the Host coming up the stairs. For the first time, she saw him clearly. His long black cloak was tattered and torn; his hood framed the wooden mask in shadow. In spite of that, she could clearly see that the mask was damaged. One red eye was gone, and the face was cracked and pitted. In the hole that belonged to the missing red orb, she could see a red and swollen brown eye staring at her. In each hand, he wielded his knives- the black blade and the silver blade, which was tinged with a reddish-brown stain.

Amber took aim and fired at his head. The shot did hit its mark, but at the distance she fired from, it just knocked his head back as it obliterated the other red eye. Blood began to trickle from beneath the mask and down onto the black cloak from the pellets that had managed to find flesh.

She pumped the shotgun and took aim once

more, but the gun jammed. She looked down and saw that a piece of cloth from her torn shirt had gotten lodged in the mechanism. Amber looked up to see the Host advancing closer, taking slow and intentional steps.

"Looks like you have a problem," he said. "Face me with no weapon, or choose to trust your friend. Who might just be with me after all."

Amber ran for the door, and the Host followed. She slid through the door and slammed it shut, then latched the lock. She looked up and saw the Host inches from her face, separated by the glass of the window. They stared at each other for a moment, her gaze locked with his bloodshot and ruined eyes.

"You know I'll get to you, right?" he said. "But I think I'll explain myself." He slammed his fist into the glass, but it held. "I have always had other...voices...in my head. But the last few years, even before Killtown, they have become ... louder. More persuasive. More forceful. When my supposed friends tried to kill me in Kingston, I took on their personas. They lived on in me. Maybe that was their intent- not to kill me, but to truly foster my growth as a killer." He struck the window again, and Amber took a step back. He continued. "The thing is, they always called me the Novice, but what they never realized, never acknowledged- was that I was always the Host. It was *my* idea, passed on to Jane Sharp without her knowing it came from me. Through an...intermediary of sorts." He slammed the butt of the knife into the window, and it cracked. Amber backed up with a yelp and hit the next door. It opened inward and she fell back into Rogan's arms. He pulled her into the recording studio and closed the door, locking it.

"I called the cops, they're on their way," Rogan said, staring out as the Host shattered the window and snaked his arm through the glass and opened the door. "The glass here is bulletproof, we should be safe until they get here."

Amber was trying to unsnag the shotgun and barely heard him. She still had her questions about Rogan, but at the moment she deemed being locked in a room with him safer than facing the Host practically unarmed. Even if Rogan had called the cops, she doubted they would arrive in time. Her gut once again churned a warning- she was not as safe as Rogan claimed. "How did the door to the studio get unlocked, Rogan? Did you leave it unlocked?" Her tone was calm and even, not accusatory, just curious.

"I must have. I'm the only one with the key besides..." Rogan looked up with horrible recognition. "Mark. My producer."

There was a tapping on the window in the door to the studio. They turned to see the Host dangling keys. Then he reached down and unlocked the door.

"Hope that shotgun is ready," Rogan said, backing toward Amber.

The door opened and the Host stepped in, drawing both knives.

"Not for shooting," Amber said as she strode past Rogan and swung the butt of the shotgun full into the Host's face. Shards of wood and the metal teeth of the saw blade grin went flying. He staggered back, and caught himself on the doorframe, then rose back to full height. The upper left quadrant of the mask was gone, exposing the raw and swollen flesh of Sean Densman's face. Another chunk was missing on the lower jaw. This allowed them to see Sean's horrific smile.

"Mark was really helpful," the Host/Sean said, his voice going in and out of the augmented tone. "He gave me a hand. And a head," he pointed the black knife to the dark corner of the room. In the heat of the moment, neither Amber nor Rogan had seen Mark's head sitting next to the microphone, his severed hand on the record button.

Amber looked up and saw that the "ON AIR" sign was flashing. Next to the sign was a camera with a green light blinking. "You're broadcasting this?"

"Of course!" the Host replied. "If I learned one thing from your mother, it is that if you want to tell the story right, you need to make it an autobiography."

Amber rushed him again, but this time he caught the shotgun as it came toward his head and he tossed Amber aside. Then he tossed the gun onto the desk that held the recording instruments. It slid off and onto the floor beneath the desk.

Rogan ran at the Host, but it was a fruitless attempt- he was met with a knife in the stomach. The Host held the other knife to his throat, and whispered, "I still need you, Rogan. I may be the storyteller, but you are the medium." He drew the knife gently across the throat, eliciting a single trickle of blood.

"As your 'medium,' I quit," Rogan pushed forward and the knife drove deeper into his abdomen. It also caught Sean off guard, and he stepped backward. Rogan slid to the floor, and Amber ran past them both.

Sean chased after her, catching her as she reached the door to the hall. He drove the knife into her back, and she screamed. Then the Host grabbed her shoulder and pulled her back into the room, pulling the knife from her back as he did. "We are not done, Amber," he said.

She scrambled back toward the studio, not really sure what her move was going to be. She grabbed a bookshelf and pulled it down behind her, slowing Sean's pursuit. She ran behind the desk and grabbed the shotgun again, wielding it once more like a baseball bat.

Sean stopped at the door, and slowly crawled over the fallen bookcase. "You know, you have a lot of fight. That's good. I respect that. And I never finished my story. See, I was born for this. I was raised in a hell the state called a foster home. I was groomed to be a killer in the systems that were supposed to heal me. And then, when I finally got to fulfill my destiny, a bunch of has-been killers tried to take me out. But I'm like you, Amber. I have a lot of fight. I built a better Killtown, and instead of it being some little unknown town, I broadcast the whole thing to my followers. They saw the hypocrites like Nikki Meyer and Pastor Casey exposed in their sin and punished. They saw the corruption of the college system laid bare and eviscerated in the body of President Straub. And that lecherous Professor Newman? The world saw how corrupt the police are when your own father shot an unarmed man at point blank range. Even if that unarmed man was a predator."

"You're sick," Amber said.

Sean tapped the small circle on his chest, a pin camera that had recorded the entire attack. "Maybe I am. But even the so-called 'heroes' are bloody in this, Amber. I learned to be efficient, quick. Dealing with all of these...people. Use some to kill for me, but even when it's just me- like it was tonight- I make the most of my time. I am just trying to purge the broken system as effectively as I can. We are all sick. And with the right push, we are all killers. My followers get that. They are going to mobilize, Amber. They are going to rise up. And even if you stop me tonight, the Host will rise. Because I am not the Host. *We* are the Host."

Amber rushed Sean once more, and the butt

of the gun again slammed into the wooden mask-directly. It shattered into a hundred pieces and fell from Sean Densman's ruined face. It was bloody and swollen, pits from buckshot oozing blood and a twisted, broken nose nearly blue from bruising.

The blow also dislodged the cloth jamming the gun.

While stunned, Amber ran past Sean once more, and this time she made it out the door. She felt a pain in her leg as a knife flew through the air and stabbed her in the hamstring. She didn't stop, but hobbled down the stairs. She could hear the heavy footfalls of Sean behind her, but she kept going. She would not let him get her. No matter what.

The Host could not win.

Her leg gave out on the last three steps and she fell to the floor face first. The shotgun slid out of her grasp a few feet across the floor, and she tried to crawl for it.

Sean reached the bottom of the stairs and tossed his remaining knife from hand to hand.

"You're going to have to kill me, Amber," he said, raising the knife for a strike as he stood over her. "Either you die, and I win. Or, I die, and I win. I will live on no matter how tonight ends. My death will only strengthen me. My followers will slay to honor me. I will be-"

"Oh, shut up!" Amber said, reaching the shotgun and rolling over. She took aim and fired.

The hand holding the knife disappeared in a

spray of blood and bone.

Sean looked at the wound with shock, and Amber pushed herself to a sitting position by the wall. "I won't kill you, Sean, but I will make sure you never hold another knife." She aimed at the other hand, but when she pulled the trigger it just clicked. Sean screamed in rage and lunged at her, but Amber brought the gun around and caught him solidly in the temple, and he crumpled to the ground, unconscious.

Amber stood over him, then pulled the knife from her leg. She stood there, looking down at Sean Densman, then she knelt next to him, placing the point of the knife on his temple. One quick push, and it would all be over. She would end him.

But that would make her like him.

Sure, the courts would see it as self-defense, but she would know. Sean was beaten, and to take his life would, as he said, grant him victory.

"I'm not going to give you that satisfaction," she said, and tossed the knife toward the door.

The hall filled with red and blue lights, and the door burst open with shouts of "Freeze!" and "Police!" One cop saw her and the unconscious man in black, and directed her to push the gun toward him.

She shoved it away with her good leg and raised her hands. She said, "It's him. He may look like Cade Faust, but it's Sean Densman."

"Cade Faust? The Detective? Didn't he kill Densman three years ago?"

"It's a looong story," she said.

◆ ◆ ◆

Rogan really had called the police, after all.

As Amber was loaded into the ambulance, she saw him being wheeled out on a stretcher, alive. She looked on, unsure if there was any hope of trust between them again. He had been innocent, and she doubted him. As he rolled by, he gave her a thumbs up. Maybe there was hope.

As the EMT dressed her leg wound, she could hear chatter on the radio. "Two live victims in the Criminal Justice building. Female in serious but stable condition. Male in critical, both en route to Memorial."

Amber looked at her attendant. "Can we go to Memorial? I think those two were my parents."

The EMT nodded. "Sure thing. Only Level III Trauma center in the region. And for what it's worth, I heard the folks working on your parents say they're going to be okay as long as they get there soon. And those guys over there can make an ambulance fly," she said with a smile.

Amber looked out as Sean Densman was wheeled out of the building, strapped to a gurney himself, still unconscious. Amber thought about what he said for the first time without the threat of death hanging over her. He said he was teaching his followers. That killing him would only make him stronger. What if surviving *also* made him stronger? What if he could keep building his cult of the Host? Had Sean Densman found a way to win, even in a loss?

Amber Knox lay on her gurney and made a decision.

She would not stop until the Host was completely and utterly defeated.

She had no idea how rash that promise would become.

Or how far the Host had spread.

EPILOGUE

Nacogdoches was in shock.

A decorated detective and three out of four SWAT members had been blown away in a trap laid by a serial killer. In addition, a local pastor, an activist, four FBI agents, a college professor, and five college students were dead. Not at the hands of a team of killers, but one singular madman. A madman who had killed another student and the University president as a warm-up.

And on top of that, the madman had been masquerading as the hero cop who had supposedly killed him three years earlier.

And they had been twin brothers.

It was ridiculous.

It was unbelievable.

It was sensational.

And the people were eating it up.

The world's media descended on the town like vultures, angling for inside scoop and answers about the Host. A name that took on new meaning, for there had been a host of identities dwelling in one man.

The survivors did what they could to avoid

the limelight. Well, most of them did.

Sullivan Knox coded twice on the table and spent a month in ICU. By the time he got out, the furor had died down somewhat. He and Lindsey, who had fared much better and was out of hospital in a couple days, made a decision to leave Texas as soon as they were both well enough. They realized that even if the horror was over, it would never be far away as long they lived anywhere near Kingston or King University. Lindsey turned down the offer to write the sequel to Killtown, but it didn't matter. The sales for her first book skyrocketed and they had more than enough to retire comfortably. They chose somewhere in rural, mountainous Colorado.

Amber was determined to fulfill her promise. She changed her major to psychology, and began to work with Dr. Crewe in the position Asher had held. At the same time, she began conducting research on dissociative identity disorder and trauma. She wanted to believe that someone could only truly defeat the Host by vanquishing the broken psyche and saving the man who had been ruined by it.

If that were even possible.

Rogan Benson also got an offer, and unlike Lindsey Knox, he took it. He got a massive advance to produce and direct the documentary he had started on, but as two movies- Killtown and Kill U. This led to a definitive split with the entire Knox family, who felt it was only going to further the schemes the Host had set in motion.

Senator King recovered from his injuries and learned of the Host's claims of a cult of followers. He immediately set out to find and eliminate all adherents to the Host's doctrines of death, using his position to mobilize a whole new unit within the FBI to seek them out.

It also began a meteoric rise of his political capital.

As for the Host- the name of the cult that the singular Host had founded- it did, in fact, grow. In the deep, dark places of the world, those who found their meaning in the machinations of the madman only became more loyal to their deity. And that is what the Host had become- godlike to his followers. They saw him as a victim of the corrupt society he had attempted to cleanse. So, they regrouped, they planned, and they prepared.

❖ ❖ ❖

Sean Densman was wheeled out of the prison hospital one week after the night of death and violence ended. He had suffered a massive concussion, tremendous blood loss, and the immediate amputation of his left hand via shotgun blast. The stump of his hand was bandaged and though he felt no pain, it ached. He had been defeated because he neither killed the girl nor became a martyr.

The prison guard pushed him down the gray hallway to the meeting rooms where lawyers would meet with their clients away from prying eyes and ears. But Sean was not meeting a lawyer that day. He was meeting a court mandated psychiatrist. A big shot lawyer out of Houston had taken his case pro-bono, and his first order of business was to get Sean declared unfit for trial. That day was to be the first day of therapy with the doctor.

The guard wheeled him in, then locked the chair in place. His hand was chained to the table, but his stump proved problematic, so the guy just left it free. Sean noted this and made a plan.

The guard left, and for a few minutes, Sean was alone.

Well, as alone as Sean Densman ever was.

The trauma had split Sean and the Host once more, but not completely.

The Host was still there, but he had been very, very quiet. Still, Sean heard his whispers. He imagined that, like Sean, the killer was wounded and healing. He would return, but it might take time.

When the door finally opened, a guard appeared and announced, "Your shrink is here."

He stepped aside and a man in a suit entered. He had board straight brown hair, parted on one side and just a bit long on the other. His small mouth was in a tight, small line until the door closed.

Then Dr. Van S. Crewe smiled. "They have assured me that there is absolute privacy, as per HIPPA and doctor-patient laws. Sean Densman, I want you to know that nothing we say will leave this room, except in the case that it serves to aid you in your defense. Do you understand?"

Sean nodded.

"It has been a little bit, hasn't it, Sean?" Crewe asked kindly.

"Since Sean Densman last met you in person?" Sean asked. "At least three years. Since just before Killtown."

"Cade Faust was, of course, seeing me regularly in the wake of his traumatic event," Crewe pointed out.

"Yes," Sean replied. "And we did have that moment at the Knox home. I trust I didn't hurt you too badly?"

Crewe smiled. "Not terribly. Hurts to laugh or cough, but a small price to pay for our plan to proceed."

"And it is?" Sean asked hopefully. "Proceeding, that is?"

"Of course. The network we created in the days leading up to and right after Killtown was strong," Crewe replied. "I knew when I met you in the state hospital you were the perfect choice to build this system around. To develop a cult of true believers who would strike out at the corrupt world around them. Sean, you have been spectacular. No one suspects just how deep our roots run."

"But I failed," Sean said, sadness at the edges of his voice. "I didn't kill her. And I didn't die."

Crewe's smile grew even more broadly. "There will be time for the final girl soon enough. As for you not dying, some out there are now spinning the story to showcase you as the wrongfully imprisoned victim of the corrupt system. That the *system* made you a killer, not trauma or biology. That almost outweighs martyrdom in the vitriol it inspires. As long as there are people that believe there is hope for your return to freedom, they will fight to make that a reality. Fight to the last drop of blood."

"So, what do we do now?"

Crewe opened his leather briefcase and slid a block of wood out. He tapped a small bump in the wood, and a wood carving knife popped out. "Should be able to evade detection. Now, you make a new Host mask. The following is already creating their own versions. They've been sharing them on the network we all created before Killtown. I'd stick close to the original, but with some tweaks. I think we can get you to a less secure location soon enough."

"And then?"

"Then we get you working on more of those gadgets like you made- the neck braces, the ChatBot and deep fake work," Crewe said, leaning back in his chair. "As far as I'm concerned, our next stage is a go. Are you in?"

Sean lifted the block of wood up and turned it in his hands. A smile crossed his still red and swollen face as he said, "Until the bitter end."

TO BE CONCLUDED...

IN THE FINAL CHAPTER OF...

THE KILLOGY

KILL U

ABOUT THE AUTHOR

Chad Lehrmann

Writer of supernatural thrillers, horror, historical fiction, and the occasional nonfiction book, Chad loves to shock and thrill his audience with fast-paced fiction and compelling characters. When he's not writing, he is a high school social studies teacher (and former minister) who loves spending time hiking in the mountains, hanging out with the family, and his pets.

Despite the content of this and other books, he wants to assure you that he is, in fact, okay.

Made in the USA
Monee, IL
01 October 2023